Summer Stories

Summer Stories

NOLA THACKER

illustrated by
WILLIAM LOW

J. B. Lippincott
NEW YORK

Library of Congress Cataloging-in-Publication Data
Thacker, Nola.
   Summer stories.

   Summary: Beginning with a lengthy bus trip and
ending with a Fourth of July sailboat ride, ten-year-
old Red enjoys both independence and companionship
as she makes her annual visit to her cousins' home on
the Gulf of Mexico.
   [1. Vacations—Fiction.   2. Cousins—Fiction]
I. Low, William, ill.   II. Title.
PZ7.T297Su 1988   [Fic]   87-45880
ISBN 0-397-32287-9
ISBN 0-397-32288-7 (lib. bdg.)

10 9 8 7 6 5 4 3 2 1
First Edition

For my mother
and for the memory of my grandmother

Contents

Summer Stories

1

South–Bound Bus

"THE BUS DRIVER doesn't like me," said Red.

She and her parents looked over at the bus driver, a bowlegged man of average height, his face made grayer by his uniform. He was standing in the door of the bus station staring grimly out across the parking lot. His gaze was fixed not on the heavens, but on a point just above the top of the bus.

"Doesn't look as if he likes many people," commented Red's mother.

"I expect *he* would say he isn't paid to like people," said her father.

"If he doesn't like anyone, I don't see why

you had to ask him to keep an eye on me. I can take care of myself."

"Because he *is* paid to do that," answered Mrs. Wilson, "more or less. And if I were you, I wouldn't worry so much about whether people I didn't see regularly liked me. Fact, I wouldn't worry so much about what people thought of me altogether."

Red stuck out her chin. "I'm not *worried*! I don't think you should make it up that I am."

"If you are not worried, and if you don't care, why are you getting mad?" her mother asked.

Her father laughed and hugged Red before she could answer back. He lifted her up to the top step of the bus. Red remembered then that she was going away for most of the summer and held out her hand to her mother. Her mother smiled and gave Red a kiss in the middle of her palm for going to sleep at night.

"Indelible. Guaranteed to last the summer," her mother told her, folding Red's fingers over the kiss. "Write to us."

"Don't fall in love, and don't make your cousins think of all the good ideas for getting in trouble," her father added. He handed Red her plaid book satchel with her lunch in it.

Red made a disgusted face at her father's advice and went to her seat. Her suitcase was already above it, where her father had put it earlier, announcing as he did every year that she could sit anywhere she liked, as long as it was the first seat behind the driver. "Just call me Hobson," her father said, and laughed. Red didn't. She didn't understand why he was laughing, and she didn't want to know.

Anyway, she would have chosen the seat for herself. Other people traveling alone often sat in the seat across the aisle and ignored the sign that said PLEASE DO NOT TALK TO DRIVER. Then the driver would ignore it, too. When that happened, sometimes Red got included in the conversation as well. But even when she wasn't included, she listened to the conversations, which were often the most interesting she'd ever heard, especially once she realized that if she looked out the window, or pretended to read, people didn't even bother to lower their voices. When she had been younger, Red had considered becoming a bus driver.

Red put her satchel on the seat next to her. Her parents walked around to the other side of the bus so she could see them waving good-bye

5

from her window. Then, hitching his pants so that he seemed to be lifting himself aboard, the bus driver climbed to his seat.

The bus heaved and rocked and began to groan out of the parking lot. Her mother stopped waving and put both her hands on her father's arm. Her parents grew smaller and smaller, and then the bus turned the corner and they disappeared from sight. Red swallowed hard against what her mother would say was a pleasurable sadness: her parents left behind, but the whole sure summer ahead of her.

Closing her eyes, Red practiced thinking of nothing at all. When she opened them again, the bus was passing the Hahl Family Dairy Farm, and the world beyond the driver's shoulder was divided by blacktop for as far as she could see. Anything could happen. And whether he liked her or not, the bus driver couldn't help but take her to Pine Level, on Onnakama Bay, near the Gulf of Mexico, where her aunt Phoebe and uncle Herman and her cousins Tralice, Joe, and Carrie Mae were waiting.

Red felt better. She reached into her satchel and brought out one of her favorite books, a biography of Queen Elizabeth I. She opened the book to the second chapter. Queen Elizabeth was only a baby princess, a disappointment to her redheaded, gluttonous father, Henry, and her unlucky mother, Anne, who both had wanted a son, although for entirely different reasons. Soon the princess would lose her mother. But no one suspected that the unwanted baby would one day be queen, and the greatest ruler England ever had.

Near the middle of the day, the bus slowed to a stop for two very thin people standing like the number eleven at the end of a dirt driveway. The health of Princess Elizabeth's younger brother, Edward, was precarious, and no one knew whom Henry VIII was going to behead next. Even though Red already knew, she hardly looked up until the new passengers slid into the seats across the aisle from her.

They were women, one much younger than the other, with noses and ears exactly alike. As Red looked them over, they turned their heads simultaneously to scrutinize her. The older one had soft gray-and-brown hair pulled into a loose puff on top of her head. Curls framed her face, which looked like a round marshmallow egg in a nest in spite of the thinness of the rest of her.

7

A plastic-pearl and silver-metal chain held glasses with upswept rims on her short nose.

Her younger companion had thick black hair caught in a severe knot on the nape of her neck. Her eyes were sharp green, with a metallic glint like a bottle top, and her face had lots of angles in it. When the older woman smiled, she didn't.

"I'm Mrs. Mildred Lucille Hunt Johnson, and this is my daughter Peach Rose. People call me Cille. Hot, idnit? You like that story 'bout Queen Elizabeth?"

Red nodded, staring. Then, slowly, she looked back down at the book open on her lap. The title wasn't showing. How had Mrs. Mildred Lucille Hunt Johnson known?

Red jerked her head back up, and was so startled to find Mrs. Johnson nodding companionably at her that she blurted out, "I'm not supposed to talk to strangers!"

That was true. But Red would usually never admit it. Besides, it was also true that she could talk to someone if the bus driver didn't object, since he was keeping an eye on her. At the moment, the bus driver was looking straight ahead, but Red knew by his shoulders that he was probably listening.

"It's okay," said Mrs. Johnson. "There's nothing to be scared of. I'm sighted. I have the gift, you might say? But I don't use it in any bad way, or listen in on people thinking. Mostly you have to pay hard attention to do that anyway, and things come piecemeal so you don't know what they mean. But books are easy. They're just out there, you understand, like overhearing a conversation. Not anything secret held close in somebody's mind." Mrs. Johnson's smile was friendly and plain. Red smiled back. This was almost as good as meeting a spy or a detective.

"How do you do?" she said politely. "I'm Nancy Jane Shoemaker Wilson, but my name is Red. Are you going far?"

Did Mrs. Johnson already know Red's name? Or where she was going? Was she really gifted, the way the fortune-tellers at the county fair every year claimed to be? Red thought she'd wait and see. After all, fortune-tellers at the fair always said the same thing over and over to everyone, and Red didn't care whether she ever met a tall, dark, handsome man. She had other plans.

Mrs. Johnson didn't seem to be aware of Red's suspicions. She answered cheerfully, "Sister, in New Orleans, is going on vacation, poor

9

thing. We're going down to mind her business for her.''

Peach Rose spoke up, her words precise as the rattle of dried peas. "My aunt Mamie Belle is an astrologer. Her clients come to her every week for consultations about their affairs, business and personal. She can't just leave them without guidance. That's not professionally responsible. She naturally makes prior arrangements whenever she goes on vacation.''

"Peaches takes after my sister Mamie," explained Mrs. Johnson proudly. "Smart, always reading and thinking. I've told her it more than makes up for—"

"I'm going to be an astronomer," stated Peach Rose. "It's a science, an *exact* science." She turned her face away to look out the window.

Mrs. Johnson kept smiling. "Peaches isn't sighted, but she doesn't take it too hard, bless her. She knows it can be a curse, and I tell you, I'm glad she's like the rest of the world. It's no help being different.''

They both waited, but Peach Rose didn't rejoin the conversation.

"Can you tell what is going to happen?" asked Red finally. "Can you tell fortunes?"

Mrs. Johnson frowned a little. "Sometimes

I can, sometimes I can't. You never can say when you're going to see, and you don't always know what to make out of it. I don't call on the gift for the fun of it, or for money either, now. Just to help out, you know, like with Sister."

"Could you tell my fortune? Could you read my palm?" asked Red.

Mrs. Johnson looked distressed, but before she could answer, the bus driver straightened up and looked balefully at Red in his rearview mirror.

"Don't you be asking Mrs. Johnson for things like that. She's told you she doesn't like to, and it's like asking for something for free, same as getting a friend who's a plumber to look at a sink, or asking a doctor's advice while socializing."

Red sat rigidly upright in her own seat and clutched the edge of it with her hands, taking a deep breath. But before she could give the bus driver her opinion of his interference, Mrs. Johnson intervened.

"It's all right," she said. "Red's sort of young to have a proper fortune. And I don't expect she'll ask me to read her palm, when she thinks of it. She's already keeping something important in it."

11

Red remembered her mother's good-bye kiss and slid quickly back on her seat. The world was a conspiracy of grown-ups, and she couldn't be too careful. She pulled her hands onto her lap, thinking, *I don't care, I don't care, I know what my future is, I'm going to the bay the bay Onnakama Bay.* The words made a singsong in her head, and when she looked at Mrs. Johnson again, she felt curiously incurious, almost light-headed.

Mrs. Johnson smiled her plain smile again and Red grinned back. Then she picked up her book so she could listen unnoticed while Mrs. Johnson and the bus driver took up the conversation.

But it was no use. Did Mrs. Johnson know Red was listening? The talk was not good bus conversation at all, just the ordinary adult kind, dull, anything interesting camouflaged in details about politics, crops, and weather. The bus driver lambasted the governor and complained of a bad back. "Hazard of the profession," he expounded. "I use up three, four pillows a year. But I've got no complaints, for all those boneheaded billy goats passing for legislators up to the state capital. . . . It's a good life, a good life."

Red waited and waited, but the conversation got no better. Mrs. Johnson never allowed anything to slip. She agreed with the bus driver, calling him captain, and when she didn't agree, she quoted the newspaper, her sister Mamie Belle, and Peach Rose, who continued to stare out the window. Disgusted, Red stopped pretending to read and went back to it in earnest.

Sometime past noon, the bus driver pulled the bus to a stop and got out. Mrs. Johnson and Peach Rose got off, too, to change buses for the one that would take them on to New Orleans.

"Have a good summer, now," Mrs. Johnson said. "To my mind, summer is the most important time of year. Don't waste it." She patted Red's arm and left before Red could answer. Peach Rose bobbed her head stiffly in Red's general direction and marched after her mother.

The shadows had folded up like umbrellas around the trees. Red realized she was hungry just as the bus driver stuck his head in the back door. "Lunch stop," he informed her. "Twenty minutes. You coming in?"

Red shook her head. She didn't tell him she had a lunch packed in her satchel.

"Suit yourself. Bus is in the shade, but you'll be hot," said the bus driver. "Cafe's over there if you change your mind."

Red watched the driver go into the cafe

13

and join two other bus drivers sitting at a table by the picture window, where they could keep an eye on the buses. The waitress appeared, and something Red's bus driver said made her laugh.

That startled Red. "I bet he didn't mean to be funny," she thought sourly. She took her lunch out and tore the paper bag in half to make a tablecloth on the seat beside her. On it she put two early peaches, small and sweet, a peanut-butter-and-cheese sandwich, and a thermos of iced tea. She drank the tea first, grateful for its musty lemon flavor and never thinking until too late how the peanut butter would stick in her mouth. She saved the peaches then, for last.

One by one the passengers filed back on. The bus driver climbed aboard. No one new sat in the seat across from Red. Soon the red earth was rolling by once more in plaits of new green corn. Herefords and jerseys and black Angus cattle grazed singlemindedly in the pastures. Horses and mules, some still in harness from their mornings of plowing and planting, rested in the shade of trees, eating their own lunches while the farmers took their noon meals inside their farmhouses. Tractors stood abandoned to the heat of the day, with grain sacks across the seats to keep them sittable.

Everything crouched down motionless beneath the sun, except the air boiling up on the blacktop and being sucked in scalding streams through the windows of the bus. Red's mouth felt dry as corn husks. She thought about the Dr Pepper her aunt Phoebe would have waiting for her. She wondered who would come meet her. Her chin slid toward her chest. Her eyes closed.

The bus had stopped beneath the sign on the Pine Level post office and the driver was reaching her suitcase down, saying, "You're here." The sun was far west, getting lower. Her cousin Joe, taller and thinner and the same brown as ever, was dancing barefoot on the still-hot cement on one side of Uncle Herman while Carrie Mae stood patiently on the other side, peering through the door of the bus.

"Come on!" Joe said. He squinted his eyes and crossed one of them.

"You've been learning important things, I see," said Red. "But you'd better quit, or your eyes'll get stuck and won't be good for anything but old blue marbles."

"Huh," Joe said. He punched her arm gleefully, pleased at the success of his trick, and smiled.

16

Red put her arms around Uncle Herman and squeezed him hard. *Families all smell alike,* she thought happily. She hugged Joe quickly and Carrie Mae longest and hardest of all.

"I'll take your suitcase," Carrie Mae offered. Carrie Mae was brown, too, and polite like Uncle Herman, but where he was very polite, and very, very polite to people he didn't like, Carrie Mae was the same polite to everybody. She wasn't talkative like Joe or bossy like Tralice or quick-tempered like Red. She thought her own thoughts quietly, and with deep stubborness. "She'd be my best friend," Red had once told her mother, "but of course you don't have to be best friends if you're already related."

Carrie Mae studied Red. "You grew. I didn't. Tralice and Joe did, too. And"—Carrie Mae nodded meaningfully—"you should see Tralice." Red nodded wisely back. She and Carrie Mae wrote letters sometimes, but it was safer to wait until they could talk.

"She'll see everyone soon enough to form her own judgments," said Uncle Herman, swinging Red's suitcase into the back of the truck.

"Ater-lay," promised Carrie Mae.

"I-ay ow-knay ig-pay atin-Lay," Uncle Herman warned them.

17

"Well, anyway, I have another surprise," said Carrie Mae.

"Oh, *those*," said Joe. Red and Carrie Mae both looked at him, and he didn't go on. Instead he leaped up on the running board of the truck next to the right front fender.

"Hurry!" he said. "Red, you can sit by the window and Carrie can sit in the middle. *I* can ride on the running board, can't I?" he finished, looking beseechingly at his father.

"Me too!" cried Red instantly. *Joe would be sneaky when he was dead*, she thought with disgust. DEAD BUT STILL UP TO SOMETHING, his tombstone would read.

"Please?" added Carrie Mae.

Uncle Herman's face grew melancholy. "Of course you can. I'm certain you are all quite capable of it. As to the question of may you—right through the middle of town? What would your mothers say?"

Joe said, "Oh," and Carrie Mae looked down, but Red said, "My mother didn't say I couldn't!"

"Absence of refusal does not imply consent," said Uncle Herman. He opened the door to the truck.

"What?" asked Red.

18

"If someone hasn't said no, it doesn't mean yes."

"It doesn't mean no, either, then, does it?" asked Red.

"In this case, it does. But we're glad to have you with us again, Red. The fine-line distinctions are not often raised with such exactitude, despite the inherent capabilities of my offspring."

Joe shook his head and got in the truck. Red and Carrie Mae followed reluctantly, but not without hope.

Pine Level hadn't changed, so Red didn't think about it one way or the other as they bumped off Pitch Street. Pitch Street, which ran straight through the middle of town from the highway to the bay, was still the only paved road. The other roads, made of sand and oyster shells, twisted and rooted back into the scrub pine and palmetto woods. Some led to other roads. Some led to nowhere. They just stopped. Red and Carrie knew those were haunted roads. Ghost alligators waited to eat people at the ends. *That* was why they were called dead ends.

Red thought of this while looking out at the light turning cool and dim among the trees, and leaned against Carrie Mae. Carrie Mae leaned back, and they rode rattling and bumping and quiet until they got to their gate. The house; the barn; George, the retired horse who shared the barn with the truck—all looked the same. The gate was open.

Uncle Herman leaned on the horn and they sailed through in one long wail. The back screen door banged and Tralice and Aunt Phoebe came out. Tralice walked with world-weary languor down the steps, but Aunt Phoebe took them two at a time. Red jumped out of the truck and ran through the early-summer evening shadows soft as water around her knees and flung her arms almost but not quite all the way around Aunt Phoebe. The summer had begun.

2

Bunk Beds

"OH, CARRIE MAE SHOEMAKER," breathed Red, dropping her satchel and suitcase in the middle of the door to Carrie Mae's bedroom. She walked slowly forward.

"That's what Joe was trying to slip and tell you, if I'd let him. I picked them out myself. They were my birthday present from everyone."

Carrie Mae had gotten bunk beds for her tenth birthday. A ladder hooked over the foot of them and a railing ran around the top one. Red had always wanted bunk beds.

Stooping, Carrie Mae picked up Red's things and brought them on into the room, but she didn't put them anywhere in particular. She was waiting to see what Red would do.

She watched her cousin scramble up the ladder and onto the top bunk. Red slid her legs under the railing and sat, surveying the room. She raised her arm straight up and touched the ceiling, then rested both arms on the rail and looked down at Carrie Mae. From where she sat, Red could see the part in Carrie Mae's hair, and the way her ears and pigtails stuck out on either side.

"You have a freckle on your part," said Red.

Carrie Mae reached up and felt her scalp. "You can't feel a freckle!"

"I can't see it, either," answered Carrie Mae. "So it doesn't matter whether it is there or not."

"Only to the antigravity people," agreed Red.

"Or birds," Carrie Mae said. "A thrush has freckles, so it might look down and think you were another thrush, if it didn't know better."

"Bunk beds," said Joe from the door.

Red rolled her eyes. "No kidding, Joe."

"I thought she should have gotten a hammock, like sailors sleep in."

22

"I didn't want a hammock," said Carrie Mae.

"How do you know? You've never tried a hammock. You could have at least tried it."

"Do sailors really sleep in hammocks?" asked Red.

"Some do. I read it in a book."

"Joe," Carrie said, "just because you read something in a book doesn't make it so."

"Well, bunk beds are okay, but someday I'm going to get a hammock anyway," said Joe.

"And sleep in the *Kite*!" Red said.

Carrie Mae and Red started laughing at the idea of Joe trying to sleep in a hammock in the little sailboat they kept tied up to the pier, but Joe wrinkled up his forehead. In another second he'd forgotten about Carrie Mae and Red altogether as he turned and went down the hall to his room, probably thinking how he could get a hammock and how he could rig it up in the *Kite*.

Red climbed down and crawled into the cave the bottom bed made. She leaned back under it. It wasn't bad, but it wasn't as good as the top bunk. Red knew Carrie Mae would let her have the top bunk if she asked for it, but she didn't

23

think her cousin was going to make the offer first. Red waited a minute, then spoke quickly.

"I like it under here. Can I sleep on the bottom bunk?"

Carrie Mae leaned forward to look at Red, but she didn't answer the question.

"It's okay," said Red. "Come on under."

Carrie Mae crawled under and propped herself against the wall next to Red with what sounded like a sigh of relief. "We can swap sometimes," she said to Red. "And you can have the bedside table. It's an old one Mama gave me, but I don't use it, sleeping up top."

Red looked over at the table. It was a good size for her books. And there was a drawer in it with a lock and key.

"You can have the drawer, too." Carrie Mae guessed, as she often did, what Red's next question was. "It's empty."

"Good." The table and locked drawer were a boon, something Red had never thought would come of being polite. But even that windfall didn't make her think she could ever be polite full-time. Politeness was one of the too many, usually inexplicable, constantly enraging things that were expected of children. But as far as Red could see, only Carrie Mae had ever come close to being truly polite. And that included all the adults she knew who were always talking about good manners.

Just then Tralice stopped in the doorway. "Haven't you unpacked yet? Mama asked Margaret Jones to come today to cook special stuff just for you, even though it's not her day to work here, so you'd better hurry up. It's almost time for supper."

"I guess when I get to be nearly thirteen, *I'll* learn how to tell time," said Red.

Tralice only smiled. "Maybe," she said, and left.

Red sent a mean smile after her oldest cousin, and began to unpack while Carrie Mae talked. Folding her socks and underwear into one of the two top drawers of the dresser, which were hers, Red wasn't surprised at all to learn that Tralice had acquired growing pains with her height.

"At least that's what Mama says," Carrie Mae told Red. "I think being taller has just made her bossier. She doesn't smack you to get her way anymore. She's got this mean look now, instead." Carrie Mae screwed up her face and twisted her pigtails into horns to demonstrate.

Red laughed, but she knew the look Carrie Mae meant. It was a family look, the same look that Red's mother had used on certain occasions for as far back as Red could remember.

"And Johnnie Brackett makes her worse," continued Carrie Mae. "You know?"

Red knew. "Johnnie Brackett's rowboat didn't sink over the winter?" she asked, without much hope.

"She's been rowing up here almost every day, even though it would be just as easy to walk. And even if she did sink that boat, she swims as good as any of us. She's been bringing over magazines, and she and Tralice sit around in Tralice's room reading them."

"Real magazines? With stories in them?"

"No, not real ones. The kind with hairstyles, and makeup, and things like that," Carrie Mae said. "Tralice got mad when I tried to look at them, too."

"Is she wearing makeup?" Red asked.

"No. She's too young, Mama says. But I think she's bought some."

"You *do*? How come?"

"Well, one day after Johnnie had left, and then Tralice had spent about an hour in the bathroom, I knocked on the door and said I had to go—because I did, that's the truth—and when I got in there, I looked in the trash can and there was all this toilet paper with lipstick and stuff like that on it. Then Tralice banged on the door and I flushed quick and left, and when I looked back in there about another hour later after Tralice got out, it was all gone."

"Wow," said Red. "She must have been in there getting the makeup off, and then she went back and destroyed the evidence, just like in a book."

Carrie Mae looked pleased at Red's reaction. "It wasn't really such a hard mystery to solve, I guess."

"Have you searched her room?"

"Nooo . . . that wouldn't be right, Red."

"Be reasonable, Carrie Mae! Detectives don't have to be polite, or how would they find anything out? Excuse me, would you please confess?"

"I suppose you read that in a book, same as Joe. I don't care. I'm not going to search Tralice's room. I didn't have to search her room to find out about the lipstick. And anyway, she'd kill us if she caught us."

"That's true," Red said. She wasn't discouraged. She had the whole summer to work on Carrie Mae. But Red couldn't help thinking it was too bad that Johnnie seemed to be having growing pains and turning useless, too. Johnnie, who was the same age as Tralice but even bossier, was every bit as good as Joe at thinking of things to do that adults had not thought to forbid.

"First call for supper," Uncle Herman called up the stairs.

Red flung her nightgown across the foot of her bed and stuffed her letter paper with the green lines and the leopard on top in the drawer of the bedside table, along with all of her best books that would fit, her notebook, and two pens, one red and one blue. She locked the drawer and held up the key.

"Why don't you put it under the mattress?" suggested Carrie Mae.

"Good idea," said Red. She shoved the key far back under the mattress. Finally, Red balanced the rest of her books on the tabletop with the smallest one on bottom, so that if they fell over, possibly in the middle of the night, they would make a terrible noise.

"Supper," Aunt Phoebe called. Red and Carrie Mae went downstairs, and Red cut in front of Tralice to wash her hands at the kitchen sink. Uncle Herman came by carrying the last platters of food. Aunt Phoebe put her hand on the kitchen doorframe, which had the years marked off summer by summer, and the heights of everyone in the family measured there for each year, with their names carefully written next to their heights. "Looks like we're going to have to make a new mark for you now that you've turned ten, Red. We'll measure you against it after supper. You've grown a good bit—almost as tall as Joe last year when he was ten. You're growing up."

"Not like Tralice, I hope," Red whispered to Carrie Mae, drying her hands.

"Shh!" said Carrie.

"What!" said Tralice, slinging the soap back into its dish.

"Did you say something, Red?" asked Aunt Phoebe.

"Nothing," said Red. She walked quickly into the dining room.

In the middle of the blue-flowered tablecloth, used on Sundays and brought out for Red's arrival, stood the mason jar Carrie Mae had decorated with shells the summer before. Now it was filled with flowers and herbs from Aunt Phoebe's garden. Red's place had been set with her favorite plate, a white china one with a wide gray border and silver scalloped edges. Almost cov-

ering the table, a platter of fried chicken, a bowl
of string beans, a casserole of creamed corn, and
a basket of cornbread sticks wrapped in a clean
blue dish towel gave up wonderful smells. Curls
of butter made a wreath around the butter in the
butter dish.

Here, it was Aunt Phoebe's turn to say
grace. At home, Red's father would be saying
grace tonight. He would sometimes say, "Good
bread, good meat, good God, let's eat," and then
add "God is great, God is good, now we thank
him for our food. Amen." Red's mother always

said, "Bless this food to our bodies and our bodies to your service. Amen." Red liked to try different prayers from Sunday school or church, if she wasn't too hungry.

But Aunt Phoebe's prayers were like long, stern conversations with God, starting with the food on the table and, tonight, thanking God not only for it, but for letting Margaret Jones be able to come fix it for them, and going on through the family, including Red and her family. She finished with a request that the world become a better place, through the God-given talents of the people in it, whose hearts should be moved not to waste them.

"For we all know," Aunt Phoebe ended, "that You help those who help themselves. Amen."

"Amen," murmured everyone, and almost before they could get their heads raised, Joe started to talk about hammocks, helping himself to a lot of the chicken at the same time.

31

3

Fish Story

RED WAS AN EARLY RISER, like her father. At the Bay, Red woke up before anyone else in the gray-blue stillness just before sunrise. That time of the day was the coolest and the noisiest: birds shouting at each other in the trees, squirrels kicking up the pine straw and leaves on the ground, and Tom irritatingly and deliberately walking from her feet to her head to knead the pillow and breathe his growling purr into her ear.

Tom, with his one blue eye and one green eye, was as fat and white as a pillow himself. He was a vain pirate cat who did as he pleased; he liked to steal or catch his food better than to eat it out of a bowl, and he liked more than anything to sit on the dock and peer down into the water. Whether he contemplated his own image or ending the lives of the fish in the murky water, no one knew. If he wasn't already on the end of the pier, he was easy to summon by baiting a hook and swinging the pole out to fish.

Stretching her arms over her head, Red pretended she was playing the piano. In the fall she would be old enough at last to begin piano lessons—to take them seriously, her mother said, and not just because everyone else was taking them. She had gotten taller, too, taller than Carrie Mae, almost as tall as Joe. After supper on Red's first night in Pine Level, when Aunt Phoebe had marked Red's new height on the doorframe to the kitchen, the mark was two inches higher than the previous year's mark.

"You'll have to borrow some of Joe's clothes to play in this summer," Aunt Phoebe had decided. "The ones you left from last year probably won't fit at all anymore." Joe had shrugged, but Tralice had said, "Oh, Mother, Red can have my old stuff. It's baby stuff anyway!"

Red had stared at Tralice in surprise, and then with the sharp beginnings of anger as she realized that Tralice was calling her a baby. She

33

couldn't help but be glad when Aunt Phoebe answered sharply, "Your offer is rude and ungracious, young lady. And the point you attempt to make about being grown becomes specious, if that is the sort of behavior you consider adult."

Tralice had half opened her mouth to answer back, Red could tell. But instead of getting into any more trouble she had, to everyone but Aunt Phoebe's regret, tossed her head and walked away.

"What's specious mean?" Joe had asked immediately.

"Ee-say?" Carrie had muttered so only Red could hear.

Starting at one end of the scales, Red crescendoed to the other, thinking about how sorry Tralice was going to be when Red was a famous pianist. Tom reared back and slapped her arm. He was ready to go fishing.

A silver-white haze overlay the pale colors of the sunrise. The day would turn hot soon, making the fish stop biting early. Red baited the hook as fast as she could, giving Tom pieces of squid from the bait jar to keep him occupied until she swung the pole out. The cork settled neatly in the water, bobbed, and went under

almost immediately. Red pulled up a small sunfish.

Tom let out an ecstatic meow that sounded
like an excited stutter.

"Fififiifish?" Red mocked him. She leaned
over, unhooked it, and let the sunfish slip head-
first back into the water. "I don't know why
you're getting so excited anyway. I'm not going
to give you a fish. Uncle Herman said fish bones
are bad for cats. And you're a cacacaacat."

Ignoring her, Tom crouched down ex-
pectantly, waiting for her to catch another fish.

Fish caught from the end of the dock were
usually too small to keep, even though they ate
a lot of bait from getting caught over and over.
By the end of the summer, Red could put almost
anything on a hook—bits of bread, leftovers, raw
peas—and catch a fish that looked familiar. Did
they recognize her, too?

Carrie Mae thought so. She would not keep
a fish to eat she thought she recognized, no matter how big it was. Or a crab either.

And she wouldn't eat meat, not even fried
chicken. She didn't like the idea of eating animals
at all. "What's the difference between eating Tom
and eating a cow?" she had asked Joe once, when
he was teasing her.

"Tom probably would taste awful," said Joe, but after that he stopped asking her if she'd ever met the vegetables she ate from the garden.

Red had laughed when Joe teased his sister. But now, like Carrie Mae, she wouldn't keep a fish she recognized, either.

Luckily, Red didn't recognize the big perch she caught just when she was about to give up for the morning. But before she could make up her mind whether to throw it back or keep it, it finned her hand and twisted loose and flopped onto the dock.

The fish never flopped a second time. Tom caught it in midair and ran.

"Tom!" exclaimed Red in amazement. Tom kept going.

Red flung down her fishing pole and ran after him as he streaked up the dock and disappeared under the porch. She skidded on her knees trying to catch him before he could get under the house where she couldn't fit. She was too late.

"Tom, come out. Come out here right now. This instant!" Red wedged herself belly down under the porch as far as she dared. She couldn't even get near him. He turned his back to her and crouched down over his catch.

"Tommmm!" yelled Red furiously. Booming in the small space, her voiced rolled out from under the house and up into the morning.

"Be quiet!" Tralice shouted down from her bedroom. "I'm asleep, do you hear?"

Footsteps passed overhead as Red backed awkwardly out from under the porch. When she straightened up, Uncle Herman was standing on the steps, his bathrobe longer in the front than in the back. He was barefooted, and he wasn't wearing his glasses. He squinted down at Red.

"What's the commotion?" he asked.

Red stared at her uncle's smooth shins and pink-creased heels and toes. When everyone went barefoot, she never looked at their feet. But she couldn't help but stare at Uncle Herman's now while she answered: "Tom stole a fish. I caught it, he stole it and took it under the house and killed it, and now he's eating it. Bones and all!"

The crunch, crunch of Tom feasting could be heard now, like the same note in a discordant scale played over and over.

"Bones and all," repeated Uncle Herman thoughtfully. "That could be serious."

Red looked up. "He's a murderer."

"He's a cat."

38

"He's a thief."

"Cats are opportunists."

The crunching stopped. It was followed by the sound of Tom scratching dirt over the remains of his breakfast for later. A minute later he crawled out and, ignoring Red, sprang up on the step next to Uncle Herman. Fish scales glittered in his fur. He licked his paw and began to wash.

Red looked back down at Uncle Herman's feet and considered what he had said. She had never thought about why fish bones were bad for cats, or how bad they might be. She said slowly, "It would serve Tom right if he just got sick and died, wouldn't it? I mean, from eating the fish bones. But he won't, will he?"

"Will Tom die?" repeated Uncle Herman. His shoulders sagged forward, making the edge of his bathrobe even more uneven. "I'm sorry, Red, but yes, Tom will die. I don't see how he can not die. No way around it."

Red jerked her head up, but Uncle Herman wasn't looking at her. He was staring down at his feet, or at Tom.

"Are you sure?" said Red. She was shocked.

Uncle Herman nodded slowly.

39

"Oh!" wailed Red. "Oh, that's not fair. Oh, no!" She leaned forward to pick Tom up, then stopped.

Uncle Herman had begun to make the odd noise, like stones shaken in an oatmeal box, that meant he was laughing. The noise grew louder and louder, until it became a real, shouting laugh as Uncle Herman fell back against the screen door. The screen bulged, and then split as if it had been unzipped straight from bottom to top. Still laughing, Uncle Herman folded backward through it and sat down without trying to save himself. Looking at his knees hooked over the bottom of the door and his feet still stuck out on the other side, he laughed harder.

"Tom's not going to die," said Red, just to make sure.

"No. At least not *now*. Stomachache, maybe," gasped Uncle Herman. "Oh, your face. I do apologize, I couldn't help it, I—"

"What's going *on*?" screamed Tralice threateningly.

"Nothing," called Red, looking at the split in the screen door and thinking what Aunt Phoebe was going to say. It served Uncle Herman right for playing such a mean joke, one that wasn't funny at all.

Then Red allowed herself a small smile. "I guess that fish was the one that got away," she said.

"Ah!" cried Uncle Herman, and he started laughing all over again.

Satisfied, Red settled herself on the steps by his out-stuck feet to wait for him to finish. Tom gave his face a last lingering, loving stroke with his paw. He gave Red a hard look. She gave him one back.

"Fish breath," she said. "No-lips."

With a satisfaction to match Red's, Tom drew himself up and jumped down to go and see what other opportunities he could find on a fine summer morning that had started so well.

4

Box Turtle

"DO YOU THINK a fish knows what a worm is?" asked Red, sliding her foot out from under the sheet to give the bottom of Carrie Mae's mattress a poke. She felt safe talking, even though it was late at night and they were supposed to be asleep. The rain, which had been falling for two days, fast, then slow, then fast, but never stopping, covered her voice and kept it from carrying beyond the bedroom.

"Carrie Mae? Are you listening? I mean, a fish doesn't call a worm a worm. How does it know it even likes worms, if worms don't live in the water?"

Carrie Mae answered slowly, her voice barely audible. "Maybe it sees other fish eating them?"

"How? Have you ever seen any worms just swimming in the water? If I was a worm, I wouldn't go near the water. And besides, *you* don't eat things just because other people do," said Red.

"No, I don't. But you do see worms out in puddles and things, after it rains."

That stopped Red for a minute. Then she said, "But they're usually drowned. The ground probably fills up with water and just floats them to the top."

"Well," said Carrie Mae. "Maybe . . ."

"What?" said Red. "Maybe what?"

"Maybe . . ." repeated Carrie Mae. It sounded as if she were wishing she could go to sleep, and forget what she'd started out to say. "Maybe worms for fish are sort of like us eating bananas when we have never seen a banana tree."

"How?" asked Red. She waited. The rain started falling harder, and a Morse code of lightening flashed through the blinds. She counted the seconds to the thunder. Good. Ten seconds. Two miles was a long way away.

"How is a fish eating a worm like a person

43

eating a banana? Carrie Mae?" Carrie Mae didn't answer, and Red fell asleep finally with the question becoming a part of her dreams.

The next morning Red woke up late, lulled by the dull steadiness of the rain. Tom was nowhere to be found. He knew Red wasn't interested in the trickling, itchy business of fishing in the rain. He wasn't, either.

Waking up late to a third day of rain made Red irritable. She quickly grew bored with everything she tried. She was already sick of mud puddles, pies, and fights. She got mad at Joe because right after lunch he ruined the jigsaw puzzle she and Carrie Mae had laid out in their room—he kept throwing pieces of it, trying to teach Tom to fetch. She got mad at Carrie Mae because she joined Joe in the attempt.

"Anyone," Red said to herself, "knows that all that cat will fetch is a fish." She went downstairs and flung herself on the braided rag rug in the den, where Uncle Herman sat, reading and reading and reading.

The bay was gray and dull as a cookie sheet. The moss hung limply on the trees. The ruts in the driveway had overflowed into one another.

"I expect to see Noah steer ashore anytime

now," said Aunt Phoebe. She and Tralice were laying out a dress pattern on the dining-room table.

"I've got a cat I could give him," said Uncle Herman, looking up from his book and making a face at the sound of Tom's meow. He looked down at Red. "And one or two other wild animals, too."

"Hah." said Red. "Hah. Hah."

Joe thumped down the stairs two at a time. "Tom's hopeless," he said. "Carrie's looking for the puzzle pieces. I helped her find a lot of them. I learned an Indian rain dance at camp. If I dance it backward, it'll work in reverse maybe."

"Washing clothes and cars is supposed to make it rain," said Aunt Phoebe, "but I don't know how to reverse those."

Joe took a long time getting the steps in backward order. The rain kept falling.

Aunt Phoebe and Tralice went back to sewing, working on buttonholes. Uncle Herman sank deeper into the armchair and read, and upstairs Carrie Mae's footsteps went back and forth as she collected the puzzle pieces with a persistence that made Red seethe inside as she lay on the rug, watching Joe watch his father.

Red knew what Joe was doing. He was

45

staring at Uncle Herman, trying to make him look up. Uncle Herman knew, too. He was sitting too still to be reading, and he hadn't turned a page in a long time.

"Excuse me," said Joe at last. "Is what you are reading interesting?"

"Yes," answered Uncle Herman without looking up.

"It's still raining," said Joe.

"Yes," said Uncle Herman.

"How many pages do you have to go?" asked Joe.

Uncle Herman put down his book and looked at Joe. "Do you want me not to read?" he asked with menacing politeness.

"Well," replied Joe thoughtfully, "I don't want you to stop reading, exactly."

"Exactly what do you want?"

"The rain to stop," Joe explained. "It's been raining forever and now it is Saturday."

"Your powers of perception amaze even your own father," said Uncle Herman. He and Joe eyed each other for a moment.

Then Uncle Herman said to Aunt Phoebe, "Suppose I go out and see if I can find the makings for ice cream?"

"I scream, you scream," began Aunt Phoebe with a smile.

"We all scream for ice cream," finished Tralice.

"It sounds like a good idea to me," Aunt Phoebe said. "I don't suppose you'll be going by yourself?"

"I don't suppose anyone would like to go with me?" asked Uncle Herman.

"I'll get my raincoat," said Joe.

Red stayed on the rug, feeling sorry for herself. When she heard the truck start, she rolled over heavily and pressed the other side of her face into the braiding, until she looked like Frankenstein's monster.

No one noticed.

Finally she got up.

"I'm going outside," she announced. "To the garden."

"Ummm," said Aunt Phoebe.

Red walked to the back door, got the umbrella, and stomped out. *I'm going out in a huff,* she thought. She slammed the back door.

The pungent, mysterious odors of the garden met her as she crossed the yard. Red leaned to ruffle the spidery dill and the rubber-leafed

47

basil by the garden fence. The smells stuck to her hands. When she got to the tomatoes, she found they were leaning sideways in the soft, wet earth. Their acrid odor surrounded her as she tightened the soggy scraps of stockings that held the plants upright on their stakes. Trying to right the stakes while she reknotted the stockings and held the umbrella wasn't easy.

"Meow." A cracked voice spoke at her feet. Red jumped. Tom stood there in the weedy grass at the edge of the garden, watching her, shaking one wet paw after the other in disgust. Red looked out from under the umbrella. The rain had stopped.

"Well, I'll be," exclaimed Red. "Good work, Tom." She tore some fresh leaves from the catnip in the hanging basket and squatted down beside Tom. He growled and swatted the leaves out of her hand, and plowed his nose into them. Then he rolled over on top of them ecstatically, forgetting the wet grass. He began to purr.

"What a silly cat," Red said. Tom fishtailed from side to side, belly up. He didn't care what she said. Red went back to work.

After tying up the whole row of tomatoes, she found the tin slug can. She went down the rows, looking for slugs and putting them in the can they kept in the garden to give to Aunt Phoebe, who would fill it with beer and drown them. Red didn't like to think about it, but Aunt Phoebe was inexorable. "The slugs will eat everything if it isn't done," she said. "And it's a painless way to go." The smell of beer always made Red think of slugs.

Something orange and black, with a piece of grass hanging from its mouth, was watching her with red eyes as she worked. She almost touched the box turtle before she saw it waiting still as a stone amid the yellow squash. When

she picked it up, the turtle pulled its head and feet back into its shell with a pop. Red put down the can and took the turtle back to the house.

Tired of looking for puzzle pieces, Carrie Mae had come out onto the porch and was drawing the pier and the bay from the perspective of the porch. The pier looked like a ladder.

"Look what I found," said Red.

"A box turtle!" exclaimed Carrie Mae. She pushed her pencil and paper away and stood up to examine it. "Come on. I bet we have a box in the pantry to put him in."

"Her, I think." Red followed Carrie Mae to the kitchen.

The pantry smelled like the garden, but dryer and stronger. Aunt Phoebe and Margaret Jones kept net bags of herbs drying there. Every few months, they emptied a different set of jars and filled them with freshly dried herbs, and put on labels with dates that Tralice wrote with green ink in script.

"Red found a box turtle," said Carrie Mae as they came back through the dining room, where Aunt Phoebe and Tralice were studying the pieces of a jumper laid out on the table. "May we have this grocery box to keep her in?"

"Let me see," Tralice commanded. She

took the turtle and turned her around and around
until Red grew uneasy.

"Give her back. She's mine."

"It's okay, Red," said Tralice. "Don't get
so excited. I'm only looking at her."

Red reached over and took the turtle, cra-
dling her in both hands. "I'm going to call her
Paint."

"You should call her Halloween, because
she is orange and black," said Tralice.

Aunt Phoebe said, "You can use the box.
She's a beautiful turtle, or tortoise, rather. Those
markings are for protection in her home in the
woods. Of course, she won't need them in a box."

"I'll fix the box up. She'll like it," said Red.

"I like Halloween, but Paint is a good name,
too," said Carrie Mae.

Red wouldn't admit that Halloween was a
good name. Tralice was too bossy to be given
that satisfaction. "Paint, her name is Paint."

"Well, you should get some grass to put
in the box with her," Tralice said. "Shouldn't
she, Mother?"

"I know that," said Red. "She's *my* turtle.
But you can hold her, Carrie Mae, anytime you
want to."

"Why don't you put Paint in the box, and

51

put the box in the corner of the porch. Then you can go and get some grass to line it with," Aunt Phoebe suggested.

"Okay," said Red. "Don't worry, Tralice. Carrie Mae and I'll take care of it."

"Honestly," said Tralice. "I suppose it's all right if I look at your old turtle?"

"Maybe," said Red. "Let's go, Carrie."

At first Paint didn't move at all. Then, as they all crouched by the box without moving or speaking, she poked her head out of her shell. She craned her neck and then pushed her way through the thick, damp grass lining her box until she reached one side. Then slowly, slowly, she turned and walked until she bumped into another side of the box. She bumped from one side to the other, over and over, until the sound of Joe's and Uncle Herman's footsteps as they came into the house made her retreat into her shell.

Joe liked Paint immediately. "Wow! A box turtle! What are you going to do with him? We could make turtle soup. I could look it up."

Carrie Mae turned to Joe in pained surprise. "You can't eat a turtle! Especially not one you know!"

"Aw, Carrie, I know that. Some people will

believe anything. I was just joking. Listen, let's go find another turtle and we could have a turtle race. Or listen, we could train this one, and put up signs and have a big turtle race, maybe for the Fourth of July picnic at the community center, and charge entry fees and sell tickets and give prizes. We could—"

"Joe, she's a box turtle, not a racing turtle, and she's mine. And she's not for dinner, either," Red said. "Her name is Paint."

"One turtle's probably not enough for soup anyway," said Joe.

Uncle Herman bent forward a little to study Paint. "A turtle in a box is more properly a boxed turtle. Do you know the poem about a robin redbreast in a cage putting heaven in a rage?"

"No," said Red. Uncle Herman's tone of voice sounded very much like Aunt Phoebe's had, and Red didn't like it.

"Hmm," he said. He turned back to the kitchen. "Come on, Joe," he said. "You and I are the kitchen detail tonight."

Red looked after them suspiciously.

"I don't think they want you to keep Paint," said Carrie Mae.

"Well, they'd better not try anything," Red said.

53

"Why would they?"

"There's no telling what people will do. They're always telling you some rule they never told you about before. I think they make them up as they go along. I do."

"Red, they wouldn't take Paint, or anything."

"Umm," said Red. She reached in and patted Paint's shell. Then she and Carrie Mae took turns helping Joe crank the handle of the ice-cream maker and watching Paint, until time for supper.

After supper Tralice shut herself in her room, announcing, with a significant look at her brother and sister and cousin, that she didn't want to be disturbed. Joe went out to look for more box turtles. The rest of the family sat on the porch as the dusk deepened into darkness.

"Ownership is an interesting, if variable, concept," said Uncle Herman to no one in particular after a while. Aunt Phoebe leaned forward.

"Are you going to build a bigger box for Paint, Red?" she asked.

"Will y'all help me?"

Red could just barely see her aunt shake

her head in the darkness. "No, I can't," Aunt Phoebe said. "It would take too much time to build a big enough one."

"How big would it have to be for one little, slow turtle?"

"Oh, something so big she wouldn't miss the woods. Something with trees and grass and rain. Turtles like to walk in the rain. You probably guessed that when you found her today. . . ."

"Uncle Herman!" Red said desperately.

"We could fence the woods," he said.

"No, we couldn't. They're not ours and they're too big and if they were fenced it wouldn't be the same for blackberry picking or forts or anything."

A breeze off the bay picked at the screens, and the swing creaked as Uncle Herman gave it a little push. Paint, feeling safe in the quiet darkness, bumped against a corner of the box.

"It isn't fair!" Red's voice rose. "George has to stay in the stable and his pasture and it's fenced, except when we ride him."

"George was born in a barn, Red. He's not a wild animal. He's lived all his life in barns and pastures, and now he's retired to the things he knows best," said Aunt Phoebe.

"Paint would get used to a box, if it were

55

a big box," said Red. "She's only a turtle. A *box* turtle."

Carrie Mae said, "Every animal is important to its own self, no matter what you say."

Red saw Uncle Herman's shadowy arm as he reached over and put his hand on top of Aunt Phoebe's. It was a conspiracy, and even Carrie Mae was in on it. The rage in Red's brain made her feel as if her eyes might roll right back in her head. She gritted her teeth. "Excuse me, I'm going to bed."

Much later that night, the sky cleared entirely. Stars and a gibbous moon appeared. The still-wet grass stood shiny as pins, and the puddles gleamed like empty new plates in the garden.

Red crouched down and put Paint under the squash plant. Water dripped off the leaves and slid down Paint's shell in glittering streaks. Red stayed still.

After a time, the shell opened a crack. Paint's head and four stumpy legs shot out. She stood up and began to walk purposefully down the garden furrow. She walked under the fence and into the tall grass at the edge of the woods as if she knew where she was going. Then she was gone.

Aunt Phoebe had told them at supper that

turtles often lived a long, long time, some of them longer than humans. Red wondered how old Paint was, and if Red was the first person she had ever seen. "Does a turtle know what a person is, even if she's never seen one?" Red said aloud, softly. "Will you remember me?"

Red's feet were going to sleep. She stood up and shook the prickly blood back into them. She picked up the umbrella she'd left in the garden that afternoon. "Good-bye," she called, and waved it. "Good-bye, old Paint." *Old Paint. Uncle Herman would like that,* thought Red. Then she went back into the sleeping house.

5

Blackberries

"BLACKBERRIES," said Red. It was a wonderful word. "Blackberries!" she said louder. *"Blackberries!"* She and Carrie Mae were walking along the pier to where Tralice was lying in the sun, to see if she wanted to go blackberrying.

"Blackberries are good," said Carrie Mae.

"Better than anything," said Red.

"Better than ice cream, or chocolate?"

"No," said Red. "That's different." Carrie Mae could be so exasperating.

"What about watermelon, or peaches?"

"I've had peaches already this summer,

and watermelon, too, Carrie Mae. So blackberries, right now, today, are best."

"Oh," said Carrie Mae. Then she said, "I like ice cream better than anything, anytime."

Red took a deep breath and shouted, *"Blackberries!"* with all her might.

"Ice cream!" answered Carrie Mae, starting to laugh.

"Blackber—"

"Zip it. Pipe down. Be quiet," snapped Tralice. She was lying on a towel on her back with the straps of her bathing suit pulled down on her shoulders. She had a slice of cucumber on each eye.

"You look like a Halloween martian." Red stared down at her oldest cousin. "A cucumber monster."

Lifting one cucumber slice to squint at them, Tralice said, "Don't be ludicrous. This is good for my eyes. It refreshes them and prevents wrinkles."

"Wrinkles? You can't get wrinkles till you grow up." Red was disgusted.

"It's not something I'd expect someone your age to understand," Tralice said.

"Cucumber eyeglasses, four-eyed vegetable face," retorted Red.

"You like blackberries, too, Tralice," said Carrie Mae, who didn't feel like getting caught between Tralice's ill humor and Red's bad temper.

Tralice closed her eye and replaced the cucumber slice on it. "Of course I like blackberries. I suppose you walked all the way out here to ask me that?"

"We're going blackberry picking," said Carrie Mae patiently. "We think they're ready, and so does Mama, and Joe's getting dressed. We came to get you, if you want to go."

"Why bother?" muttered Red. Both of them ignored her.

Tralice sighed, but she sat up, took the cucumber slices off her eyes, and sailed both pieces into the bay. "Oh, all right." She rolled her towel up carefully, pulled her T-shirt over her bathing suit, and at last said, "Let's go."

Red turned and sprinted toward the house, trying to run on the most weather-bleached boards on the pier because they absorbed the least heat. Carrie Mae, who had worn flip-flops, waited for her sister.

A truly beautiful woman, Tralice had told them once after reading the *Home Guide to Beauty*, always walks with dignity and confidence, her head held high. Now Tralice walked slowly down the pier, trying not to look at her feet. Stealing admiring glances at Tralice's pink-glazed toenails, Carrie Mae paced beside her, keeping step, until Red could stand it no longer.

"Puh-lease," she said. "Come on!"

"I'd hate to see what I'd have to wear to go outside in the winter if you could pick blackberries then," said Red to Carrie as they pulled clothes out of the drawers. For picking blackberries Aunt Phoebe always insisted that everyone wear long-sleeved shirts, blue jeans, thick high socks, and high-top sneakers laced to the ankles. She gave them old gloves, too. Only hats were optional.

"It's a pain," said Carrie Mae, but she didn't really seem to mind. She put the hateful, heavy clothes on quickly. "Aren't you ready yet, Red?"

"In a minute," said Red. "You go on— I'll be right down." The past winter, Red had had an idea, and the time for that idea had come— unless Aunt Phoebe was smart enough to take the one last chance Red offered her.

"Do we really have to wear all this stuff?" she called down over the stair rail.

61

"Oh, Red," said Carrie Mae from the stair landing. "You know what Mama'll say."

Sure enough, "Wear them," Aunt Phoebe called up, loudly and sternly. "No ifs, ands, or buts."

"Yes, *ma'am*," answered Red sarcastically, but only so Carrie Mae could hear her. In a normal voice she said, "You were right, Carrie Mae."

Going back into the bedroom, Red took out her bathing suit and put it on. If Aunt Phoebe was going to make Red be sneaky, then it wouldn't be Red's fault. She'd given her aunt every chance, hadn't she?

Red put everything else required for blackberrying on top of the bathing suit and examined herself in the mirror. The one-piece bathing suit was like thick underwear. Red decided she didn't feel one bit guilty.

But not feeling guilty didn't make her feel any cooler. By the time she joined her cousins on the porch, she was sweating all over and beginning to feel annoyed in spite of her plan. The *slip-slip-slip* of the fan through the hot air goaded her on.

"Why do we always have to wear all this

junk?" she asked, throwing her gloves into her bucket.

"I told you," Aunt Phoebe said in a warning tone of voice. "I do not want to nurse any of you through a case of summer poison ivy or, Lord forbid, snakebite."

"I've never gotten snake bit or poison ivy," said Red.

"See how well my system works?" Aunt Phoebe said, smiling, but her tone of voice said, *Don't push your luck, young lady.* Joe and Tralice laughed, while Carrie Mae, who was always quick to know how someone was feeling, turned diplomatically away to pick up her bucket.

"Good luck," said Aunt Phoebe. "Now go on—I've got work to do."

With Tralice leading the way, they set out on the long walk to the blackberry patch.

Red decided to wait until they got there to show everyone what she'd done, so Tralice wouldn't run back and tell. Tralice, Red reflected, would tell soon enough anyway, but Joe would be envious of Red for thinking of it. "I'm surprised *you* didn't think of it, Joe," she would say. All in all, it would be worth it. She put thoughts of Aunt Phoebe out of her mind.

Tralice had forgotten about practicing her *Home Guide to Beauty* walk as she led the way down the road and along the shortcuts through the fields and woods and bits of marshy ground. She slapped her bucket against her leg and whistled. Joe thumped his bucket against everything he passed, hoping to make a snake jump out. Carrie Mae walked alongside Red and tried to cheer her up. Carrie's kindness only made it worse.

"You'll forget about how hot you are when we get there," said Carrie Mae.

"Boy, will I," said Red nastily. She knew Carrie Mae was hot and sweaty, too. Why wasn't her cousin upset at how unfair things were? It wasn't right.

Tralice stopped whistling. "It's something you can't change, Red. You're only being silly, you know."

Same to you, only more of it, thought Red, but she didn't answer.

Joe kept looking for snakes; snakes weren't as dangerous as Red when she had lost her temper. Letting Red walk and stew in her silent rage, Tralice, Joe, and Carrie Mae began to talk around her. That made Red even madder, and the madder she got, the hotter she got, and the hotter she got, the madder it made her. By the time everyone got to the blackberry patch, Red felt as if someone had poured boiled ice cream down inside her clothes. Not even the sight of the loops of blackberry canes bent under ripe blackberries made her feel better.

"Look!" shouted Joe, sending the birds feeding on the blackberries up into the trees with his voice. "Let's race to see who gets the most!"

Like he doesn't say the same thing every year, thought Red scornfully, watching Joe run to get a head start. Tralice and Carrie Mae raced after him. Soon they were all shouting and laughing and throwing squash-ripe berries at each other. They ate two for every one they picked.

Red neither ran nor shouted. She trudged among the bushes, stripping the berries from each one methodically. She didn't look up, and she didn't put a single berry into her mouth. But surprisingly, she couldn't quite muster the courage to show off her bathing-suit idea.

"Watch out!" Joe threw a blackberry at Red.

"Stop that!" she screamed.

"Baby," taunted Joe. "Why aren't you more *mature?*"

65

Tralice laughed. "Oh, Joe, I don't sound like that!"

"I am not a baby! And you're a worse one, besides!"

"Red—" said Carrie Mae. She didn't get to finish her sentence.

"Shut up!" said Red, unforgivably. "Leave—me—alone." She turned and stalked away from them.

When she was good and far away, and calmer, she dropped her bucket and wriggled out of her clothes. Then, in her bathing suit, rolled-down socks, and high-top sneakers, she began to pick blackberries on her own.

The coolness felt wonderful. *I'll pick a million blackberries*, thought Red. *They'll be sorry.*

Gradually, the bucket grew heavy with blackberries. It was easier to pick them without sleeves and gloves to catch on the thorny branches, but now the blackberry prickles stuck in her hands and arms. She picked her way deep into the clearings of the woods, where the air was dense and humid and the insects swarmed around her, taking bites. Soon, for every blackberry she picked, she was taking a swat at a horsefly or a mosquito or something unidentifiable but undeniably hungry.

"Whew." Red put her bucket down and

plunged her hand into a new thicket of black-berries jeweled with fat, perfect fruit.

But her hand wasn't alone. Something jumped beneath it. Red screamed and flailed backward. She stumbled over the bucket and sat down hard as a king snake sliced out and headed for safety, as scared of her as she was of it. But even after seeing it was only a king snake, Red couldn't stop screaming. She screamed all the air out of her chest twice before she could stop.

Only when she caught her breath did she realize how quiet everything was. No one had come running to see what had happened. Her cousins were not crashing through the under-brush to save her.

"Hey," called Red. No one answered.

"Hello?" she called. Her voice disappeared between the trunks of the trees.

Then Red felt something sticky beneath her. "I'm bleeding!" she thought. "I've been snake bit and I'm going to die!" She looked down. She was sitting in blackberries, blackberries oozed up between the fingers of one hand, the crushed blackberries had turned her into an insect feast. Mashed blackberries spilled from her overturned bucket were scattered on the ground all around her.

Red scrambled to her feet. She pulled a handful of leaves from a sycamore tree and wiped the blackberries off as best she could. Then she gathered the berries that weren't crushed. They barely covered the bottom of her bucket.

All that work! All that time spent picking blackberries and not eating a single one. Red lifted the bucket and threw it against a tree. The rest of the blackberries flew out. "So what?" said Red. Her plan was ruined anyway. If she didn't bring back a lot of blackberries, she'd just look dumb, standing there in her bathing suit. She'd have to get her clothes and put them on, and use her idea another time.

All she had to do now was to try and stand how awful it would feel until she could take a bath, and to try and think of an explanation for having no blackberries at all.

She needed a new plan, but first she had to find her clothes.

Red picked up her bucket and started back through the woods. She went down one hill and up another, from clearing to clearing, where the blackberry bushes grew. But before long all the clearings began to look alike. Red stopped. Where were her clothes? And where was everybody else?

"Hello?" she called. The minute she heard

her cousins' voices, she could get her bearings. "Hello?"

No one answered. She kept walking, and even the things that looked the same didn't look familiar.

"Great. Just great," said Red. She raised her voice. "Hello," she called, and then, "Carrie Mae! Joe! Tralice!" over and over. She wasn't answered by even an echo. "Help!" she tried at last, but it was no use.

Red sank down onto a pine log. She was too disheartened to care anymore about the insects, even the ants that appeared as soon as she sat down. She pulled off a pine splinter and held it to her nose and took a deep breath.

She was lost.

"God," she said to herself, and then stopped. You couldn't bargain with God, Uncle Herman said. When the time came, you usually weren't in a position to negotiate anyway. She understood now what he meant.

Nevertheless, Red took a deep breath. "PleaseGod, let me find my way back, and I'll try not to lose my temper anymore. Much. Except for good cause."

Nothing happened. Red brushed the ants from her leg, slapped her neck, and felt a little calmer. She tried to make her mind a blank, so she wouldn't distract herself by crying. And then, snaillike, a thought crept up into the blankness.

The sun rose over the bay from the left every morning as she fished. It went down on the right. Red saw it suddenly, as if she were standing on the end of the pier. And if that was so, the house faced south. So somewhere to the south was Onnakama Bay, because to get to the blackberry patch they had walked left—east— from the house, and then turned left again off the road—north. Somewhere to the south, then, was the bay, and if she could find the bay, she could get home.

Relief filled Red. She knew it was past noon, with the sun going west. By keeping the sun to her right, she would be sure she was walking south, and sooner or later she would come out on the edge of Onnakama Bay.

"And then," said Red aloud, "I'll have to go around behind Johnnie Brackett's house so she won't see me like this." There was nothing, Red was sure, that Johnnie Bracket would like better than to see Red and ask a bunch of questions and then tell on her, as soon as Johnnie got the chance.

Red picked up her bucket again and stood

up. "Thank you, God," she said. She started to walk.

She walked and slapped and scratched and sweated, but she made herself think only of going south. She'd wash off the blackberries in the bay, if she could just get there.

Finally, finally, she came to one of the oyster-shell roads. She was so relieved, she walked out to the middle of it and took comfort in standing there. She felt as if she had never been so tired in her whole life, and she let her knees give way. Someone, sometime, had to come along the road and help her. This time her mind went blank of its own accord.

She didn't hear her cousins until Tralice was squatting down, putting her hand on Red's head to raise it, and then pushing her bangs back as if she were Red's mother or Aunt Phoebe, checking for fever.

"Where have you been?" demanded Joe.

"Shhh," Tralice told him. "Red, are you all right, honey?"

Red began to cry, and she didn't pull away when Tralice put her arms around her saying, "Hushhh, shhh, it's okay."

"My clothes are gone," choked Red.

"It's okay."

"We found them," said Joe. "We thought you were running around *naked*. Or in your underwear. We went back to look for you because we didn't mean to lose you, exactly. . . ."

"Hush!" Tralice said.

Red lifted her head. "You left me!" she wailed.

"Oh, Red," said Carrie Mae. She was starting to cry now, too.

"Oh-hh," sobbed Red. "And there was a k-king snake and all the bugs bit me and I was lost and I lost all my blackberries and Aunt Phoebe will kill me!"

"I don't think Mama'll do anything like that," Tralice said. "We have plenty of blackberries—don't worry. Here, use your shirt to wipe off all that stuff you've got all over you. You're a mess. We'll take the road all the way home, so you won't get scratched up anymore. It'll be easier walking, too."

Tralice stood up and held out her hand, and for once Red was glad her oldest cousin had a take-charge nature. She was relieved not to have to make any decisions.

73

"You left me," she said again, but she took Tralice's hand and got up obediently.

Carrie Mae picked up Red's bucket. "We just moved a little ways away from you," she said, "because you were in such a temper. You weren't any fun, and we thought we'd find you after you had had time to get unmad."

Red didn't answer. She walked next to Tralice without speaking all the way home.

"Good heavens!" cried Aunt Phoebe as she saw them come through the gate. She pitched down her rake and seized Red. "Are you all right? You didn't get snake bit? Come here, don't talk!"

She undressed Red and made her stand under a hot shower. Then she poured witch hazel over her arms and legs and rubbed it into her neck. Red burned all over. Then Aunt Phoebe put her into bed.

Red's punishment for being deceitful was to stay in bed for the rest of the day, without seeing anyone. But she didn't mind so much. She thought she'd never seen anything so good as the glass of iced tea with mint her aunt set on her bedside table, or felt anything so good as the cool, clean sheets being pulled up around her.

"I'm sorry," said Red, just before Aunt Phoebe closed the bedroom door.

Aunt Phoebe nodded. She didn't look quite so forbidding. But she didn't say it was okay, I told you so, I hope you learned your lesson.

She left Red to figure that out for herself.

6

Blackberry Cobbler

RED LOCKED THE DRAWER in her bedside table and slid the key back under the mattress. She got onto her bed and leaned against the wall with her box of leopard-decorated paper on her knees. It was after lunch, and hot, and she didn't feel like doing anything, so she had decided to write a letter home.

She tried to remember what the teacher had said about writing letters in school the past year. Before that, Red had discovered, she had been writing letters all wrong. Now she wrote the date at the top right-hand side of the paper and stopped. Then, although she called her parents

Mama and Daddy, she wrote, as she had been taught, "Dear Mother and Father." She paused, then wrote quickly: "How are you? I am fine, thank you. I hope your summer is fine without me. We go to church every Sunday. Tom ate a fish I caught, but he won't die. We have a lot of blackberries we picked. Someone is going to make blackberry cobbler soon, I hope. I will see you soon. Love, Nancy Jane Shoemaker Wilson (Red)."

She reread the letter and thought about blackberry cobbler. She had thought about it off and on all day, through blackberries on her cereal at breakfast and blackberries with sugar and milk for dessert at lunch. She'd said at lunch, "We have lots of blackberries still for cobbler."

"That would be good," Uncle Herman had said, laying his napkin beside his empty bowl. "Blackberry cobbler is my favorite."

It's my favorite, too, thought Red. *Why doesn't someone* do *something?* She put the letter in its matching envelope and took it down to the hall table for Uncle Herman or Aunt Phoebe to mail.

Carrie Mae came through, on her way to read on the porch swing.

"Blackberries don't keep very long," Red said.

77

"I know," said Carrie Mae.

"You don't know how to make cobbler, do you Carrie?"

Carrie shook her head. "Of course not. Do you?"

"What do you think?" said Red. "I guess I'd better do something about getting some cobbler made, before all the blackberries go bad."

"We could always go pick more," Carrie Mae said.

Red didn't answer that. She didn't like the idea of going blackberrying so soon after everything that had happened on the last trip. Instead she said, "Why do I have to do *everything*?"

"You sound like Tralice," said Carrie Mae. "But good luck." She went onto the porch.

Red went to look for Joe and found him propped against a tree in George's paddock, reading, while George stood nearby, one ear back and one ear forward, his eyes half closed.

"Joe," said Red.

"I'm reading," said Joe.

"Have you ever read about how to make cobbler?"

"You were talking about that at lunch, and I don't know how to make cobbler, and I've never read about it."

"Wouldn't you like to know?"

"I'd like to read about how to do it, but there are other things I'd rather be doing. Like reading, right now," Joe said. Punching Joe would be nice, thought Red, but she had to keep in mind that she might need his help later on for something. Punching him wouldn't change him, anyway.

Joe bent back over his book, and when George leaned a little closer and plucked Joe's shirt between his lips to see if the book might have turned into something good to eat since the last time he checked, Joe didn't even look up.

Red left them and went to look for more likely allies.

Tralice and Johnnie Brackett had the *Kite* upended in the front yard. They were scraping paint off her, a process that, Red knew from past experience, was endless.

"Blue trim for the Fourth of July," said Tralice. "You should help."

Red stopped at a safe, unhelpful distance. There was plenty of time to get ready for the Fourth of July. "Blue reminds me of blackberries. Don't you think some blackberry cobbler would taste good—if the blackberries haven't gone bad?"

"It sure would. Is someone making some?" asked Tralice.

"Someone should be," replied Red.

Johnnie Brackett laughed, an ordinary laugh instead of the shrill trill she and Tralice practiced from the magazines. Red didn't mind too much.

"We're going to start painting soon, and besides, we're on diets. Why don't you make some cobbler? Then I might have a little bowlful, even."

"Me! Johnnie Brackett, you are no help. You and Tralice are the ones who are always reading magazines. Don't they tell you anything useful, like how to make cobbler?"

"Why can't you do it yourself?" asked Tralice. "Why should we have to do everything?"

"Good-bye," said Red. "I'm going to talk to Aunt Phoebe."

Tralice shrugged and went back to her work. But Aunt Phoebe only said, "I'm busy. Talk to Margaret Jones. If she's got time, she might help you out. She's in the kitchen."

Red knew Margaret Jones was in the kitchen. She'd been avoiding that end of the house altogether because of that, and she didn't like her aunt's suggestion at all.

*   *   *

Margaret Jones was the only person Red had ever known who didn't make general conversation. She didn't tell stories and she didn't make jokes. She didn't talk about the weather, how are you doing, my how big you've grown. She didn't fill up the air with words. She stuck to facts or silence.

Red didn't understand it. Red didn't understand how Margaret Jones could be a grown-up and be that way.

Once, when Red was little, Margaret Jones had caught her sitting on the floor of the pantry, eating out of the jar of sweetened condensed milk she had sneaked out of the ice box. The tall, broad shape had suddenly filled the doorway just when Red had been thinking that her aunt and Margaret Jones were far away in the top of the house working on the windows. Red had dropped the jar with a cowardly squeak and made a break for safety. But Margaret Jones had caught her easily and held her at arm's length to examine her.

"You have tapeworms, child?" asked Margaret Jones.

"No!" cried Red, trying to slither free.

"Then you've got no business eating this stuff. It's pure sugar, and worse'n a grown man

81

with liquor." Stepping to one side of the pantry door, Margaret Jones gave Red a little shake and dropped her. Red shot through the door, but before she got away, Margaret Jones administered two stinging smacks on the seat of her shorts.

"Don't let me be catching you again, you hear?" she said, punctuating the last two words with her hand.

Red fled without daring to answer or look back. Margaret Jones had never told on Red, but on the other hand, Red didn't think Margaret Jones saw much use in her after that, either.

All in all, Margaret Jones made Red uncomfortable.

Red couldn't do what her aunt suggested. Instead of going to the kitchen to find Margaret Jones, she went back to Carrie Mae.

"No luck?" asked Carrie Mae, who had listened to Red's conversation with Tralice and Johnnie from the porch.

"Joe's reading, too, and won't stop, and doesn't know how to make cobbler, either, and Aunt Phoebe said ask Margaret Jones," Red told Carrie Mae. "I give up."

"Why? It can't hurt to ask," said Carrie Mae. She never had understood why Red avoided Margaret Jones.

Carrie Mae had always liked Margaret
Jones, liked the smell of the kitchen when it was
full of her cooking, and liked the way her hands
moved surely, ceaselessly in their work. Red
thought her cousin also liked the quiet Margaret
Jones kept, a quiet in which Carrie Mae, stub-
born and silent herself, felt comfortable.

They looked at each other, and Carrie Mae
suddenly realized that Red was afraid of Margaret Jones! "Come on," said Carrie Mae aloud.
"We'll go and see."

In the kitchen, Margaret Jones had everything from the shelves and cabinets ranged around
on the floor. She was reorganizing.

"Hi," said Carrie Mae. Red stopped a little
behind her cousin and didn't call attention to
herself by speaking.

"I'm fine, thank you," said Margaret Jones.
"Now what is it you two want?"

"We picked some blackberries a little while
ago," said Carrie Mae.

"I saw."

"They need to be made into blackberry
cobbler. Will you do it?"

"I won't," answered Margaret Jones. "But
I'll tell you how."

Red was too surprised at this to object even

when the next thing Margaret Jones said was "Put on some old clothes first."

But as soon as they were out of earshot, Red complained, "Every time you have anything to do with blackberries, you have to change clothes."

Carrie Mae laughed. "It's true," she said.

When they got back, Margaret Jones tied aprons around their necks even though they'd dressed in their oldest shorts and shirts. Then she told them to get out the blackberries.

"Wash 'em and put 'em in the big pot on the back of the stove."

Carrie Mae and Red obeyed, picking through the blackberries and eating the ripest ones as they washed them.

"Well, how do they taste?" she asked them when they'd finished.

"Medium sweet," said Carrie Mae. "Would you like some?"

Margaret Jones shook her head. "Put sugar on them. You," she addressed Red, "would like them real sweet, but there are others to think about." Before Red could think of anything to answer, she went on. "Then, after sugaring, turn the fire on low."

Red let Carrie Mae add the sugar while,

under Margaret Jones' sharp eye, she got out the flour, baking soda, salt, shortening, and buttermilk, and the measuring cup and spoons. Before she would let them do anything else, Margaret Jones made them measure out the amounts they would need of each thing.

"Now, Red, sift together the flour, soda, and salt. Carrie Mae, spread out a handful of flour—you'd better make that two—on that board over there."

Red shook the grit left over from sifting into the garbage and handed the bowl to Carrie Mae.

"Put the shortening in, a little at a time, until it feels like a handful of peas. Work it between your fingers. . . . Now, add a little buttermilk until you have a nice smooth dough," instructed Margaret Jones. All the time she talked, she kept lining the shelves with fresh paper and arranging the jars and cans to her satisfaction. Still, she managed to know just when the dough had turned pea textured, and when the right amount of buttermilk had gone in. When the dough was smooth enough for her, Margaret Jones gave it an approving slap that made Red shift uncomfortably.

Then Margaret Jones pointed to the rolling

pin on the counter. "Rub a little flour on the rolling pin so it doesn't stick, and roll out the dough, about as thick as three nickels. Then you'll take a knife and cut it into strips and weave them crisscross on the cobbler."

Taking turns, the two girls did as Margaret Jones said. Twice she had to stop and help them. Her hands moved as quickly as Red could blink.

"When will the blackberries be ready?" asked Red.

"When they swizzle," answered Margaret Jones. "And you'll know when that happens."

Margaret Jones went on with her work. Red and Carrie Mae stood by the stove waiting for the blackberries to be ready.

"A watched pot never boils," said Margaret Jones to nobody in particular.

"Or swizzles, either," whispered Red.

"Or swizzles," agreed Margaret Jones.

At last the blackberries began to roll in their juice. Hot purple foam boiled up the sides of the pot with a sissing sound.

"They're swizzling!" cried Red.

"They are." Margaret Jones looked over and nodded. "Work fast! Weave the dough like I told you, across the top of the pot, and push each layer down until you've used all but one layer's worth. That goes on top for the crust.''

With Margaret Jones' help, they put the pot in the oven, to let the crust on top brown. "Hurry," said Red to the oven. She and Carrie Mae crouched down to look at the cobbler through the glass window on the oven door. Margaret Jones wouldn't let them open it until she said it was done.

Red thought she'd never seen anything so wonderful as the cobbler they lifted at last onto the top of the stove. The rich, purple smell of it filled the kitchen and spilled over into the whole house. As Margaret Jones set the pot on the trivet on the table, Carrie Mae could only say, "Oh, boy, oh, boy," while Red made herself dizzy taking deep breaths of the pungent steam. "The air tastes like blackberries," she said.

Joe appeared in the kitchen door. "Something smells good," he said.

"Awfully good," said Johnnie Brackett's voice behind him in the hall.

"Wonderful, in fact," said Tralice. "Mama, come here!"

"Well, well," Aunt Phoebe said. "I'm impressed."

"Say, 'Thank you,' " said Margaret Jones.

Carrie Mae looked surprised and a little

hurt. "I was going to—" she began, but Red interrupted her. For the first time since she'd gotten caught when she was a little girl, Red looked directly at Margaret Jones. "Thank you," she said, and smiled. Margaret Jones didn't smile back, but she nodded.

Red looked around. "Thank you," she repeated. "We don't mind if you do have some, do we, Carrie Mae?"

They dished it up and served it around.

"It's the best cobbler I ever tasted," said Aunt Phoebe after her first bite.

"It's a little sweet," said Margaret Jones.

7

The Sign at the End of the World

AUNT PHOEBE PAUSED in the back door, and the pause was a pose. Her white straw hat with the silver and green leaves was tilted over one eye, and her dark hair was anchored with silver combs. She wore a dress the soft green of the leaves on her hat, with white carved buttons. Clipped on her ears were round silver earrings, like moon shells.

As she walked down the stairs and took Uncle Herman's arm, she did not look down at her feet, or at her children and niece sitting under the canopy rigged over the back of the truck for Sundays. She looked only at Uncle Herman.

Aunt Phoebe is vain! thought Red. And hard on the heels of that thought came the realization that Uncle Herman mattered the most to Aunt Phoebe, more than the rest of her family. It was a strange thought, but it was not one to think about just then, in the truck on a Sunday morning going to church. She put it away as they drove through the gate.

"Just once, I'd like to go somewhere in decent style! I wish we could trade this old truck in for a real car," said Tralice. "I bet we could afford it, and you can haul hay and stuff just as easily in the back of a car. Other people don't have to look so ludicrous and conspicuous going to church."

"Church. Who cares? Who cares what you look like? This is *my* favorite part of going to church," Red said to Carrie Mae. "The best part."

Carrie Mae braced herself with her legs to keep her balance on her place on the upended book box, carefully keeping her hands folded on her lap so her gloves would stay clean.

"No one's saying anything, because it's true," Red said.

"So what if it is?" asked Tralice. "You think Mama would let us do anything else on Sunday?"

Red sank back next to Carrie Mae.
"No," she said.

New fans in the hymnbook racks on the backs of the church pews depicted two golden-haired children playing near a cliff, while a pink-and-golden angel stood between them and the edge. In small letters at the bottom was printed "John 3:16" and "Grace Funeral Home."

Red contemplated the scene. The children didn't look like they were playing at anything interesting. Always blond, pink angels and blond, pink children. Blond. Where were the redheaded angels?

She waved the fan furiously and squinted to see if she could make the children seem to move, but she couldn't fool her eyes. Then Aunt Phoebe gave her a look. Red stopped and sighed, but quietly.

Red liked singing hymns, but there were only three throughout the service, not counting the Doxology at the end, or the choir's music while the offering was passed. In the summer, the choir tended to stick to unfamiliar, antiphonal hymns that could be safely carried by one or two good voices, so the lack of a rousing bass

and confident soprano section wouldn't be noticed. And the stained glass, in Red's opinion,
was not nearly as interesting as that in her larger
church at home. No, decided Red, the chorale
didn't count as a hymn, and if the meek were
going to inherit the earth, she was not going to
be among the heirs—unless being a child made
one automatically count as the meek. The way
grown-ups went on, you'd think it did.

Red rolled her eyes as far sideways as they
would go to look at Carrie Mae. Carrie Mae
wouldn't whisper in church, and usually seemed
to be good without trying, or being a pain about
it, and yet, Red's thoughts ran on, she knew in
her heart that Carrie Mae wasn't one of the meek
either.

She and Carrie Mae were so different, but
they had not being meek in common. Maybe they
had other things in common, too, which meant
Red wasn't all that different from a person so
surely good. Maybe everyone in the world was
more connected like that, in good ways under-
neath. Thinking this gave Red a sense of hope.
Being meek wasn't the only way of being good,
and being good didn't mean being just like other
people. There were peacemakers and all sorts of

93

others included in the Beatitudes. Red thought, *Maybe I can be one of those.*

The minister stood at the door of the church afterward to shake hands with all the members of his congregation, except for those too young to resent, or resist, having their heads patted by him. Red sidled out on the far side of Tralice, who had been graduated, apparently, from head patting to hand shaking. Red had to admire Tralice's poise.

As they gathered in the shade by the truck, a miracle happened—Tralice came up and said, "Mama and I are riding home with the Bracketts in their car. We'll meet you back at the house."

Carrie Mae and Red looked at each other and looked away. Each knew what the other was thinking: Would they get to ride on the running board of the truck, even though they were in their Sunday clothes?

"*May* we ride on the running board? Please?" begged Red as Uncle Herman came up to the truck.

Uncle Herman didn't even pause as he opened the truck door. "It seems to me we've had this conversation before, and—get in the truck, all three of you—it seems to me I said it would be impossible to let you ride on the running board through the middle of town."

Red, Carrie Mae, and Joe squeezed onto the front seat of the truck and waited until Uncle Herman had pulled away from the church.

"What about when we're not going through the middle of town?" asked Joe.

"Hmm," said Uncle Herman. He bumped the truck off the tar onto the oyster-shell road that wound its way to their house—and away from the center of town.

He cleared his throat.

"There's a road," he began, "over in Louisiana, down there in a swamp. I don't need to tell you about swamps, I know—"

"Swamps are areas that—" began Joe.

"Buzzards, snakes, and quicksand!" said Red happily. If they couldn't ride on the running board, Uncle Herman's telling a story would do almost as well.

"Alligators," said Carrie Mae.

"Mosquitoes," Joe said lamely. "Mosquitoes multiply in stagnant water."

"And that's not all," said Uncle Herman. "Think of all those green lagoons of still water, where the wind never blows and more than just

95

mosquitoes thrive. *Some*thing makes the trees creak and moan and the surface of the water quake."

Midday shadows on the road shivered over the truck. Spanish moss and sawgrass brushed against the doors and tires. Red looked out at the sulky light pressed hot against the ground, like something waiting to happen, and inched away from the door, to lean against Carrie Mae.

"Well, I was walking on this road through this swamp in Louisiana. Snakes slithered away underfoot, buzzards made passes like swing blades circling overhead, mosquitoes were thick as flour, and I knew if I stepped off the path it would be into quicksand or an alligator's jaws."

"Why were you there?" asked Joe.

"Joe!" Red said.

"That's another story. . . . Anyway, the more I walked, the narrower the road got, and the more the trees grew together overhead until they were laced tight like bootstrings. And then everything got dark, dark, even though it was the middle of the day, and the darker it got, the quieter it got, until there wasn't even the sound of buzzard wings or alligator jaws. And the mosquitoes had disappeared. Completely."

"Why didn't you turn around?" Joe broke in again.

"That's part of the other story," Uncle Herman said. "Now, I kept going. I kept going until all of the sudden I came up on this giant tree dead center of the path. It had bark like human skin, and it seemed a face looked back at me out of the trunk. And right there, up above what looked like a face, nailed to the tree, and something dark oozing out where the nail went in, *there* . . . it . . . was. . . ."

"What?" cried Joe.

"The Sign," Uncle Herman said. "The sign that said, 'The End of the World.'

97

"Well, the terrible thundering in my ears was my heart. It had my blood moving so fast, my knees locked and I couldn't fall down and faint. Because you see, I'd heard about that half-human tree holding up that sign. You couldn't find it by looking, people said, but once you came upon it, you never came back. You couldn't get away, couldn't turn around, no escape.

"And since the sign marked the very end of the world, no one could say what was on the other side. There were no maps. . . . Some said treasure, more treasure than Aladdin could conjure, more incredible than Alice could find through her looking glass, were across the edge. Others said it was another planet where worse than cannibals caught you and fed you to their children, one finger and toe at a time. But whatever was on the other side of that sign, whether you meant to cross over or not, just seeing it meant the end of you. Forever. There was no going back."

Uncle Herman took the last turn to their house.

"Well, I looked that sign over good. Didn't touch it. Then I leaned around the tree and tried to look past it without getting too close, you know. But there was nothing to see. Green water, green trees, gray-green mist, and long gray moss trailing down onto what *might* have been more road.

"I looked behind me. And even though it was pitch dark in that direction now, I decided I had to make a try at going back the way I came. I turned.

"And then I heard it."

No one dared ask.

"Someone, or something, was coming soft and slow and steady up the road behind me, coming up the road toward me through that awful darkness, coming closer, closer, closer. . . ."

Carrie Mae forgot politeness. She grabbed Red's arm, and as Red jumped roof high, Carrie Mae shouted, *"What did you do?"*

"Do? I *ran!* I jumped around that tree and felt the bark grab up against me, but it couldn't keep hold. I closed my eyes and ran right past the tree and the sign and on over the End of the World."

Everyone was silent as Uncle Herman pulled to a stop in front of their gate.

He looked at them. He shook his head sadly. "And you know? I never came back."

Carrie Mae let go of Red's arm, Red straightened up, and Joe began to frown.

"Hey," said Red. "That's not fair!"

"Is that it? That's all?" asked Joe.

"Say something, Carrie Mae," said Red.

"It was a good story," said Carrie Mae, "but—"

Uncle Herman forestalled her. "If you're going to complain about it being a tall tale, I make the claim that height has nothing to do with truth.

"Now, everybody out. Red, push the gate open for me. Y'all step up on the running boards, hang on tight, and fly off quick as we get around the barn, or it'll be the end of the world for me!"

Red opened the gate and ran back to jump on the running board by Carrie Mae. Joe braced himself on the other side by Uncle Herman. They swung down the driveway and around the edge of the barn and jumped off fast as the back screen door banged.

Tralice stood there, swathed in an apron, her hands on her hips.

"It's just about time someone got here to give me some help with dinner! Where on earth have you been?"

8

Rabbit Tobacco

"I WONDER where everybody is," said Red.

"Who cares?" Carrie Mae kept her eyes on the fish head dangling from the piece of string she was holding over the edge of the pier. She and Red had been trying in vain to catch a crab all afternoon.

"Who cares?" Carrie Mae said again, bitterly.

That day, after lunch, when Uncle Herman had come out the back door carrying a grocery list and the book box with books to go back to the library, Carrie Mae had been waiting. *"Through the Looking Glass,"* she had reminded

101

him, jumping up off the bottom step. "You won't forget, will you?"

Tralice, who had held the door open for Uncle Herman, had started to laugh. *"Through the Looking Glass,"* she'd mimicked, letting the door slam to underscore her scorn. Johnnie Brackett, who had just gotten there, had joined in the laughter.

It was too much. On top of not being able to go into town to the library that day herself, because Uncle Herman was going to be in court over at the county seat all the rest of day, it was just too much. Carrie Mae had lost her temper. "Stupid lipstick faces," she'd screamed into the shadows of the house. "You'll be sorry, *sorry*."

The pitch of Carrie Mae's voice had yanked Red, who was trying to herd a centipede into a stock corral by the side of the house, out of her concentration, and Carrie May herself had yanked Red up before she could even protest. Clutching Red's hand, she almost flew out to the end of the pier.

"I just hate Tralice," gasped Carrie Mae. "She's as mean and ugly as a—a—catfish!"

Still thinking somehow about the centipede, Red almost made the mistake of saying that a catfish wasn't really ugly, but she caught herself in time. Instead, looking at her cousin's pinched face, she had said as soothingly as she knew how, "I'll go get the fish-head bucket and the crabbing stuff, and we'll crab off the end of the pier."

"Time to start getting ready for supper, I guess," said Carrie Mae. She pulled the string up, untied the fish head, and dropped it back into the bay.

"Now!" said Red, looking down into the water. "*Now* there are crabs. I bet they were watching from under the pier all afternoon."

She and Carrie Mae contemplated a large, mossy-looking crab that had slid out of the shadows to box the fish head between its claws.

They both looked at the crabbing net, but they knew it would be useless. Then Carrie Mae shrugged. "That crab looks sort of familiar anyway, so we couldn't have kept it." She stood up and picked up the bucket. Red gathered the net and string and followed her to put everything away. As they came to the barn, Tom materialized to inspect the net and strop himself against the fish-head bucket.

"Ha," said Red. "No crabs, no fish heads. Nothing. That's what you get, fish thief." She trailed the string for Tom to chase and almost ran into Carrie Mae, who'd stopped dead.

"Shhh, Red! Do you smell that?"

Red sniffed. "Something burning?"

"The barn!" Carrie Mae dropped the bucket and ran.

But it wasn't the barn. The inside of the barn was quiet and smelled only of hay. They could see George in the paddock just beyond his stall door, dozing in the last edge of sunlight.

"Listen," whispered Red. An indistinct murmuring, as elusive as the smell of smoke, came from the back of the barn.

"That's where everybody is," Carrie Mae whispered back. "Behind the barn. Come on."

They crept toward the back of the barn. As quietly as possible they shifted a bale of hay aside and lay down next to each other in its place. They peered through a ragged, narrow gap between three of the boards and the floor of the barn.

Almost directly in front of them Joe, Tralice, and Johnnie Brackett were sitting in the stubbly grass amid cut-up scraps of paper bag and the stalks and stems of the gray, dusty weed, with the narrow leaves that looked like rabbit ears, that Aunt Phoebe called rabbit tobacco. They had the kitchen matches.

"You see?" Joe was saying. "I told you

that you could smoke rabbit tobacco. Same as cigarettes, only free!"

He brandished his twisted, half-burned paper-bag cigarette, but he didn't relight it.

Johnnie Brackett's words came slowly. "Why didn't you tell us sooner, Joe?"

"Research," said Joe. "These things require research. You can't just— Hey! You don't look so good, Johnnie."

"I don't feel so good, either," she answered.

"You're a funny color, too."

"Am I?" Johnnie lifted her hands to her face as if to check the color. Then she looked at Joe.

"Oh, Joe! You're kind of a funny color yourself."

Tralice, who had lain down flat, spoke. "I think I'm going to throw up." She held her lips still when she spoke, like a ventriloquist.

"That does it," hissed Carrie Mae. She jumped up and raced out of the barn. Red ran after her and once again almost collided with her as Carrie Mae stopped, put her hands on her hips, and shouted, "You better not be sick, Tralice Shoemaker! Daddy will be home soon, and it's your turn to help fix supper!"

"Carrie!" shrieked Tralice, bolting up. She raised her hand to her mouth and fell back.

"Are you going to tell?" asked Johnnie faintly.

"Don't be ludicrous," said Carrie Mae. "I don't care what *you* do."

"I think I have to go now," said Johnnie. "It's getting late." No one tried to stop her as she cautiously got up and left, propping herself against the barn with one hand as she walked.

"Phew!" Red wrinkled her nose. "That stuff smells worse than burned cabbage!"

"I'm going to die," moaned Tralice.

"You'd better not die, either," said Carrie Mae. "It's suppertime now."

"I don't think I'm going to die, but I can't help with supper," Joe said.

Carrie Mae bent to pick up the kitchen matches. "I guess you do believe everything you read, Joseph Butler Shoemaker. Like some fairy book. Like *Through the Looking Glass*. And I suppose you'll do anything you're told to do, Tralice, if Johnnie Brackett says it's okay. Smoking! And lighting matches by the barn!"

Turning, Carrie Mae marched back to the house. For the fourth time that day, Red followed her. Everything was all mixed up.

Carrie Mae put the matches back on the stove just as Aunt Phoebe came into the kitchen.

"What are you doing with the matches, Carrie Mae?" she asked sharply.

"I knocked them off the stove," Carrie Mae said, her face closed. "Red and I swapped with Tralice and Joe. We're going to help with supper tonight, and they're going to clean up."

Aunt Phoebe gave them both a thorough onceover, but she only said, as she opened the pantry, "You can start by setting the table, then."

Uncle Herman lowered a book with the word *Remedies* stamped in gold lettering on the spine. Bits of scribbled paper littered his desk.

"Come in," he said. "What can I do for you?"

"This is serious," said Carrie Mae. "We thought we'd talk to you first, since you're a lawyer, and since Mama is busy."

Uncle Herman looked at his jumbled desk. For a moment he looked the way he had when he'd told Red that Tom was going to die. Then he said, "Well, if that's the case, you'd better sit down."

Carrie Mae and Red cleared a space on the sagging old chaise lounge and sat down.

Red waited. She wasn't exactly afraid, but she was a little in awe of the set of Carrie Mae's chin. During supper, Red had almost believed that she could feel the heat of Carrie's outrage. Afterward, Carrie Mae had only said to Red, "Come on," and Red had come. A seldom-lost temper, Red realized, was a truly awesome thing to behold.

"Well?" asked Uncle Herman.

"Tralice, Joe, and Johnnie Brackett were smoking behind the barn today. We found them smoking rabbit-tobacco cigarettes, made with pieces of paper bag. They had the kitchen matches," Carrie Mae said bluntly.

Her father sat back and pressed his palms together. "Well-ll," he said.

"What are you going to do?" Carrie Mae demanded.

"I don't know," answered Uncle Herman.

The last bit of Carrie Mae's self-control escaped her. "What do you mean, you don't know! You're supposed to know! What about smoking! What about the barn! What about the matches! What about *everything*!"

"Everything?" asked Uncle Herman, but Carrie Mae didn't hear him. Gripping the arm of the chaise lounge so tightly that half-moons of purple appeared under her fingernails, she screamed, "Tralice is awful. All she ever does is make fun of me. 'Go away, you're just a child. Don't be ludicrous, Carrie Mae. How could a mere child understand anything?' Who does Tralice think she is? She's horrible, and she's never any fun anymore!" Carrie Mae's voice had risen to a shriek. She fell back, gasped, and to Red's amazement began to cry.

Uncle Herman got up and came around his desk, but Carrie Mae turned her face away from her father. "Go away," she sobbed. "And don't say it's all right." Uncle Herman stopped in surprise, but he obeyed, and leaned against his desk instead.

"I won't say it's all right. What Tralice— and Joe and Johnnie—have done is serious, very serious, and wrong. In fact, it sounds as if Tralice has committed a lot of serious offenses.

"But two wrongs don't make a right, and the spirit in which you are telling me this is wrong, too."

"You're not going to punish Tralice, or any of them, are you?" asked Red. She put her hand on Carrie Mae's shoulder and kept it there, even

though Carrie Mae gave a half-hearted shrug as if to pull away.

Uncle Herman stretched his lips and showed his teeth, but it wasn't a smile. Red wanted to look down, but she didn't, even when Uncle Herman said, "You'll make a lawyer yet, Nancy Jane." Red willed herself not to move, or look away, although her heart had begun to pound hard. Carrie Mae stopped crying and began to scrub at the tears on her cheeks with the back of her hand. The desk lamp made a cage of light that kept them all in, and the everyday sounds of dishes being washed and put away, crickets singing rounds, the persistent two notes of the mourning doves, came from far away.

Uncle Herman moved first. He stood up. "I can punish Tralice and Joe—and notify the Bracketts—and you will get your revenge. But under the circumstances, I'm not sure you'd find it satisfactory."

"What circumstances?" asked Carrie Mae. She swallowed hard.

"Whenever people live together there are ordinary wrongs, misunderstandings, differences of opinions about how things should be done and why. Manners and laws take care of some of these problems. Sometimes these—rules of civiliza-

111

tion—even prevent the problems. But some problems can't be prevented, some things can't be avoided or changed."

Carrie Mae nodded. Red watched her uncle warily.

"If you think about it, you will realize that some of the things Tralice is doing are not characteristic of her. And although you could blame Johnnie Brackett, I think you'll realize that it is a willing army that makes the general."

"She does it because she wants to, not because Johnnie talks her into it?" Red blurted out.

Uncle Herman really smiled at her this time, a small, rueful smile.

"But why?" asked Carrie Mae.

"Inevitable. It means no matter what you do, a thing will happen. The sunrise is inevitable. Becoming an adult is inevitable. You can't stay a child forever, and that is what Tralice is learning. Everyone has to. Some people try not to, and never get past the first part. Other people, if they are lucky, or smart, keep growing inside all their lives. But whatever happens, the first part is the hardest part, I think, because you aren't a child and you aren't an adult, and you don't really understand the rules, and you don't know what to do."

"I'm not going to be like Tralice," said Carrie.

"You'll grow up," said Uncle Herman, "but maybe it won't be so hard for you. For one thing, you may have learned something from Tralice. Do you understand?"

"No," said Carrie Mae.

"No," said Red just as stubbornly.

"Do you want to?" he asked softly, and he walked back around to his side of the desk. The cage of light became a lamp on a desk once more, and the sounds became part of the air again.

"Then look at it this way, you two. Tralice is the oldest. She is used to being in charge, and she is used to being right. Now she isn't sure of herself anymore. Maybe she's not smart enough, maybe there's something wrong with the way she acts or looks. That's what she thinks, and she's scared, sometimes, and she's mad, sometimes.

"But whatever she feels, she tries to pretend she knows what is going on, and at the same time she tries to be as much like everyone else as possible. It's a camouflage, protective covering—that way, no one notices if she doesn't act

113

right. That's why she imitates people who act more confident, like Johnnie. But that isn't what Tralice is really like, and she knows it. And acting against her true self makes her unhappier. She takes it out on other people, particularly those who can't fight back. And that, incidentally, probably makes her feel worse."

"We can't fight back," Carrie Mae interrupted, her voice desperate.

"What are you going to do, then?" Abruptly, Uncle Herman seemed to be through with what he'd been saying.

"Me!" Carrie Mae was shocked.

"You." Uncle Herman nodded. "Why don't you try to talk to Tralice, about how you feel and how she feels. See if you can work things out among you."

To Red's astonishment, instead of telling her father what a bad idea that was, Carrie Mae got up. "Thank you," she said. She stuck out her hand, and when her father leaned forward and took it, they shook hands.

"You're welcome," said Uncle Herman. He seemed pleased.

Red kept her hands in her pockets. She didn't say anything.

*   *   *

Back in their bedroom, Red climbed up the ladder to the top bunk bed, drew back her fist and gave the ceiling a good, hard thump.

"He should have done something! He kept talking about rules, and being adult, and then he doesn't do anything when Tralice and Joe and Johnnie go and break an important rule. It's not us who are always breaking the rules, it's them, the grown-ups. . . . Does he really believe we could talk to Tralice?"

Carrie Mae came up onto the top bunk next to Red and leaned her chin on the rail. Her face was as blank as her father's could be.

"Carrie? You don't think we should try to talk to her? Do you? It'll only make her mad."

"No. I know. Adults"—she stressed the word as if it were a bite of something sour—"talk a lot, don't they? Even when you don't know what they're talking about. Maybe they can't help it, but it's no wonder Tralice acts so weird, if she's headed in the same direction!"

Carrie Mae went on, thoughtfully. "We could try to talk to her, like Daddy told us to. Do you always believe everything they tell you? Parents and teachers and preachers?"

Unexpectedly, Red remembered her mother leaning over her bed one night, stroking her fore-

115

head. "Your father and I still love each other," Red's mother had said, and the arguing voices that had wakened her had faded and she had gone safely back to sleep.

But now Red realized that she knew better than that. She herself didn't love anybody when she was angry, she didn't love them again until she was over it, and where else had she gotten her temper from but her parents?

Red took a deep breath. "No," she admitted. "I don't believe everything adults say."

"No? Cross your heart and hope to die?"

"Stick a needle in my eye," answered Red. She drew a cross over her heart and raised her hand shoulder high, palm out, to show she was telling the truth.

"Well, then," said Carrie Mae, "what are we going to do?"

"Listen," said Red at last. "I don't think we should tell Tralice we told Uncle Herman and that he's not going to do anything. We'd be worse off than ever. She'd think she could do anything. Instead, I think we should tell her that she's headed in the wrong direction. The wrong direction," Red said again, enjoying using a phrase

116

she'd heard her mother use, "and if she doesn't start acting right, we're *going* to tell."

Carrie Mae considered the idea. "It might work. But we should be careful about what we want her to do to keep us from telling on her. After all, if she can't help it, what good does it do to ask her to act right?"

"We're not asking her. She doesn't have a choice," said Red. "But you're right. We'd better just ask for important stuff."

"All right then, she can't call us silly or ludicrous or children ever again. And she has to tell Johnnie that she can't either," said Carrie Mae. "And if she doesn't want to do something with us when we ask, she can just say no, thank you. Or else."

"Or else," said Red.

"Or else," said Carrie Mae to her sister. "Joe, you're a witness to this, and that's why we're not telling on you, either. You'll help—"

"Enforce it," said Joe.

"Yes," said Carrie Mae. "Enforce it."

It was the same night, just before bedtime. Tralice, who had been locked in her room ever since supper, stood across from them, with Joe halfway between, and Carrie Mae and Red at the door, which they'd pulled shut behind them when they'd knocked and asked to come in.

"Do you agree?" asked Carrie Mae. She stuck out her hand, just as she had with her father.

Tralice looked funny. She blinked hard, and Red thought she saw tears in her oldest cousin's eyes.

But there were no tears in her voice when she finally answered.

"I agree," she said. "But don't try to get anything else on this deal. That's it. You understand?"

"Oh, Tralice!" said Carrie Mae.

"Understand!" said Tralice harshly.

"We understand," said Red, "if you do."

"Joe, you're in this too, just as much as I am," said Tralice, "so don't try to get away with anything."

"Not me! Let's shake on it." Joe pumped Carrie Mae's outstretched hand once, then Red's, while Tralice watched without moving. Joe looked relieved; pale, still smoke sick, but relieved.

Carrie Mae started to lower her hand, but Tralice stepped forward. Her fingers closed around Carrie Mae's and she held them for a minute before she gave Carrie Mae's hand a quick, brief shake. Then she took Red's hand, too.

"I can't believe it," said Red.

"Me either," said Carrie Mae.

"I didn't think it would work, Carrie Mae."

"Me either."

"You don't think being like Tralice is inevitable, do you?"

Carrie Mae looked back at the door to Tralice's room, which she had just closed behind them.

"No," said Carrie Mae firmly. "I think it's just bad luck. It only happens to some people."

9

Joe Goes Swimming

AUNT PHOEBE had long ago written the rules out and posted them by the back door. The curling, yellowed paper read:

1) NO SWIMMING FOR AT LEAST ONE HOUR AFTER EATING ANYTHING.

2) NO SWIMMING, SAILING, OR ROWING ALONE.

3) LIFE PRESERVERS MUST BE WORN IN BOATS AT ALL TIMES.

The rules had been there so long that no one read them anymore, and no one complained very much about having to obey them. Aunt Phoebe, of course, didn't have any trouble following the rules, since she didn't mind wearing a life jacket and since she never, ever went swimming.

"Too much work," she always said. "And I'm allergic to getting sunburned."

Aunt Phoebe meant what she said. Whenever she was outside for long, she wore a long-sleeved shirt, long, loose pants, and a hat—a floppy hat tied under her chin for crabbing and fishing and boating, a wide, stiff straw hat for gardening, and a stiff-billed canvas hat for working in and around the barn, as well as special Sunday hats.

Red's nose peeled from the beginning of the summer to the end, and she got freckles enough for a second skin. Joe and Carrie Mae turned red-brown, like Uncle Herman. Tralice, with Johnnie Brackett, worked on a scientific tan while lying in the sun on the pier in bathing suits, slathered with baby oil and iodine. But Aunt Phoebe stayed pale as buttermilk.

Then one morning, Joe was late to breakfast. He didn't sit down at the table until the first plate of biscuits had been eaten and Uncle Herman had gone to get a second.

"I'm sorry I'm late," said Joe. "But I think you should know that I'm not eating breakfast.

121

And since I am not, I can go swimming whenever I want."

Joe paused triumphantly, but Aunt Phoebe didn't jump in with an argument about the importance of breakfast. Instead she said, "I don't like to eat breakfast myself," and poured herself another cup of bitter chicory coffee and milk.

Uncle Herman returned and set the biscuits on the table. "Who doesn't like breakfast? Someone on strike against my biscuits?"

"He's not eating!" Carrie Mae said around a mouthful of grits. She swallowed hastily. "Sorry. I didn't mean to talk with my mouth full."

"Don't worry," Uncle Herman said. "This calls for desperate measures! Joe?"

Joe's face reminded Red of Tom's when he'd stolen the fish as he said, "If I don't eat, I can go swimming whenever I want!"

"Ah. And how long do you propose to adhere to this regimen of starvation in the pursuit of aquatic endeavor?"

"What?"

"How long do you think you can go on not eating?" snapped Tralice. "Until you're so skinny you can't float?"

Red thought hard and fast. Joe was up to something again, and once again he'd gone ahead

with a good idea and deliberately not told anybody. He was a sneak, and worse, he'd probably
take the rowboat to the middle of the bay to
swim, or sail the *Kite* so far no one else would
ever get to sail again.

As if he'd read her mind, Joe said, "I'm
going swimming any minute now, or maybe I'll
sail to the middle of the bay to dive."

"That's not fair!" said Carrie Mae. She
stopped. Red was wriggling her eyebrows up and
down and reaching for a biscuit.

"Ummmmmm." Red took a big bite of
biscuit. "These are just delicious. Uncle Herman, they're the best biscuits you ever made."

The biscuits were good, but they weren't
that good. Carrie Mae was puzzled. Then, suddenly, she understood what Red was doing.

She reached out and selected two biscuits
for herself. "They look so good, I think I'll have
more," she said. Red grinned.

"And they smell wonderful, don't they
Carrie Mae?"

"The best smell in the world," said Carrie
Mae.

A small silence fell over the breakfast table
as Red and Carrie Mae chewed and swallowed.
Then Tralice smiled evilly and drew the plate of

biscuits over. She took two, made a pool of sorghum syrup and butter on her plate, and began to dredge her biscuits slowly through it.

"These biscuits are excellent," said Tralice. She took the bowl of grits and ladled out the last spoonful. "But these cheese grits are just as good, Mama. Joe, I'm so sorry you had to miss this—but I think Red just took the last biscuit."

Aunt Phoebe made an odd noise and hastily began to drink her coffee.

"Everything is extraordinarily exceptional, eh?" said Uncle Herman. "Please note, Joseph."

Joe took a deep breath. "I can't think what to do first, while y'all sit here eating and eating. May I be excused?"

"A hot, clear day," Aunt Phoebe reminded him. "Be sure and put on lots of lotion. All of you."

"You will all have lots of time to put plenty of lotion on," Joe said, paying them back. "And you won't have to worry about washing it off for a good while."

Hateful! thought Red. *Plain hateful.*

"I'm excused?"

Aunt Phoebe nodded.

Joe stood up.

124

"Wait a minute!" Tralice said. "Joe—I'm so sorry, but you can't go swimming after all." She picked up her last bite of biscuit and finished slowly as Joe began to sputter.

"I can too. What do you mean? I didn't eat anything. Everybody saw me!"

Neither Red nor Carrie Mae minded the maddening calm with which Tralice finished her biscuit. It was worth the wait.

"It doesn't matter whether you ate or not," said Tralice at last, as if she were speaking to a very small child. "You can't go swimming—or out in the boat—by yourself. Can you? It's the rule, isn't it, Mama?"

"That's not fair!"

"It is the rule," said Aunt Phoebe. "And it is not one that will be broken."

"It's a stupid rule," said Joe.

"Watch it," said Uncle Herman.

"Watch what!" shouted Joe, glaring at his father.

"And don't look at me in that tone of voice, either," said Uncle Herman sharply.

With an effort, Joe made himself look down. Red felt almost sorry for him, even though it served him right for being low and selfish with

125

a good idea. She forgot all the other times that Joe's ideas had gotten her into trouble when he had shared them.

Aunt Phoebe set her coffee cup down. "Joe. I'll go swimming with you. I didn't eat any breakfast, either."

Everyone, even Uncle Herman, was too startled to speak. Joe's eyes went from furious catlike slits to wide-open surprise.

"Well. Well." Uncle Herman cleared his throat. "Now that is something I'd like to see." He smiled at Aunt Phoebe, and for some reason she looked down, smiling faintly to herself. "But I have to go see a man about a suit."

"A suit?" asked Red, who should have known better.

"A *law*suit!" said Uncle Herman. He took off the old tablecloth that he'd made into an apron and hung it by the door as he went out, laughing to himself.

Aunt Phoebe got up, too.

"But you never go swimming!" cried Carrie Mae. "Never!"

"But I have." Aunt Phoebe gestured vaguely. "And now I am again. I'll go get ready, Joe. We'll go off the pier, if you don't mind."

"Mind?" said Joe. "I guess not!" He turned

and raced out of the room to put on his bathing suit.

"I guess he doesn't have to help clean up, since he didn't eat," said Tralice. Glumly, she and Red cleared the table while Carrie Mae scraped and stacked the dishes and put them in the sink to soak.

"I don't believe this," Red said.

"Talk about unfair," said Tralice.

Carrie Mae didn't say anything.

They finished in the kitchen and went out to the back porch to wait. But no one was prepared for what they saw when Aunt Phoebe came out. Her audience froze with shock as she walked by and started down the pier toward Joe.

Tralice recovered her wits first. "Honestly," she said, "no wonder I don't remember ever seeing Mama swim. I must have just put it out of my mind completely," while Red bit the insides of her cheeks and tried to think of sad things to keep herself from laughing, and Carrie Mae forgot her feeling of betrayal. She hung a forefinger on each side of her mouth and pulled down hard to keep her face straight. Even Joe seemed struck dumb.

Aunt Phoebe's bathing suit was completely hidden by one of Uncle Herman's long-sleeved shirts, buttoned almost to the top. The shirt came down past her knees. She tied her floppy fishing hat on her head and put on old white going-to-church gloves.

Carefully, she climbed down the ladder into the water. Still speechless, Joe leaned over and handed her an inner tube. She slipped it over her head and floated gently away from the pier.

Joe looked back at the house. His voice returned.

"Yaaaaaaaaaaaaaaa!" He backed up and ran off the pier in a cannonball, full speed.

Red couldn't help it. She was mesmerized by the sight of Aunt Phoebe in the water, and the next thing she knew, she was standing at the end of the pier, looking down.

"You really are allergic to the sun," said Red.

"Very." Aunt Phoebe was floating in a puddle of shade made by her hat.

"Look at me!" Joe climbed out and did another cannonball, and then again and did a can opener.

"Very good," said Aunt Phoebe.

"What happens? About the sun, I mean," asked Red.

"I break out in a rash, and I might swell

up like a balloon. My eyes and throat might even swell shut."

"Worse than the time Red got so sun-burned she was covered with blisters and sick and had fever?" Carrie Mae and Tralice had come up behind Red. Red didn't think it was necessary for Carrie Mae to bring up something embarrassing that had happened when she was little and couldn't help it. Not necessary, and not polite.

"Much worse," said Aunt Phoebe.

"You'll never be able to get a tan!" Tralice said.

"No," answered Aunt Phoebe uncon-cernedly.

"Look at me!" Joe said, and he bobbed upside down to try and tread water with his feet in the air. Aunt Phoebe only nodded as he came up spluttering. She pushed off again from the pier and flutter-kicked a little ways into the bay.

"I've seen enough. I'm going inside." Tralice raised her voice. "Be careful, Mama! Be careful in the sun!"

Aunt Phoebe waved placidly.

They set up the Monopoly board on the screened porch.

"I don't think I'm going to go swimming today," said Carrie Mae.

"Me either," said Red.

"Make that three of us." Tralice counted to Reading Railroad. "I'll take it."

"Doubles and Free Parking," Red told the dice.

They'd forgotten about Aunt Phoebe until she climbed the steps. She looked even odder with her clothes wet. Red couldn't help it. She snickered, and that set her off laughing. But Aunt Phoebe didn't seem to mind.

"Whew! That felt good. It's been too long." She hung her soggy hat on an outside nail peg and pushed her hair back. Joe came slowly up the steps behind her, rubbing his hair with a towel.

"It's been more than a good hour since breakfast. Y'all could go swimming if you wanted to," Aunt Phoebe said.

"No, thank you," answered Carrie Mae, concentrating on the game. Tralice had, as usual, managed to get all the green properties, knowing full well that they were Carrie Mae's favorites.

" 'Take a ride on the Reading,' " Red read in disgust.

"Pay me," said Tralice. "I own all four railroads."

"Want to go swimming?" asked Joe.

"Nah," said Red. She began counting out tens and twenties and fives to pay Tralice. Tralice hated small change.

"Feels great," said Joe. "Wasn't Mama neat?"

Carrie Mae drew a card and read, " 'Get out of jail free.' "

"Don't drip on the board, Joe," Tralice said.

"I almost did a full flip off the pier!"

"You can't buy the electric company, Red. Tralice owns it," Carrie Mae pointed out.

"Anyone want to go sailing?" Joe asked.

"Snake eyes," Tralice said with satisfaction.

Joe sat down.

"I could keep the bank for you," he said.

"It's too bad there aren't any biscuits left," said Tralice. "Being a big property owner makes me hungry."

"Not being one makes you hungry, too," Red said. "Pitiful, I'm doing pitiful."

"You could trade with—" Joe began.

"It's nice of you to share your ideas with

us *now*, Joe. But now we don't need them," said Red.

Joe closed his mouth.

The game went on.

Joe was so quiet that Red could hear him being quiet. Joe was almost never quiet. He liked to talk. He said things aloud to see if they were true. If he read something he thought was interesting, he thought everyone would be interested. He could make up whole commentaries about whatever he was doing, like the baseball announcers on the radio.

But, Red remembered, he had been quiet on the long trip back from picking blackberries, when she had lost her clothes and her blackberries. And he hadn't made fun of her about it once since then. Joe respected a good idea, even when it didn't work. Was it so terrible if he had one that he didn't share, if he outsmarted them now and again?

Yes, it is, she thought. *I won't look at him. I won't feel sorry for him.*

She looked over at Joe where he sat, still and quiet, and her mouth said his name anyway and there was no going back.

"Joe."

Joe kept still.

133

"You can keep the bank."

Joe scooted forward, but Tralice stopped him with a shake of her head.

Carrie Mae looked at Tralice imploringly.

"No," said Tralice. "Anyway, I'm getting tired of Monopoly."

"Well, I'm not," said Red.

"Tralice—" Carrie Mae pleaded.

"Let me finish." Tralice looked at Joe sternly. He stayed where he was. "*I'd* like to go swimming."

"Oh," Red said. "Okay."

"Okay," agreed Carrie Mae.

Tralice fixed Joe with a look. "You're welcome to join us."

"It *was* a good idea," said Joe.

They all looked at him silently.

"It was," he insisted. "And if I'd told you what I was going to do, you never would have gotten to see Mama go swimming."

"Joe," said Carrie Mae.

"All right! Okay!" Joe jumped up.

When he was safely out the screen door, he called back, "I'll wait on the pier, but hurry, will you? It's almost time for lunch!"

10

Fireworks

"AND A FINAL REMINDER," intoned Reverend Calvin, "of the annual Fourth of July picnic to be held at the Pine Level Community Center from noon onward, weather permitting, which we will leave in the hands of the Lord, concluding with fireworks, to be supervised by the volunteer fire department, as soon as it is reasonably dark enough."

He raised his hands, and the choir launched into the Doxology.

Red let out a sigh. No one needed to remind her of the Fourth. In the middle of the summer, the end of it began. She'd been at the white house on the edge of Onnakama Bay since the first week in June. She would go home the first week in August. Each summer she thought the Fourth of July would never come, and each summer it did and then the time after that went twice as fast.

Later that afternoon, after Sunday dinner, she gloomily watched Joe check the flattened tin cans he'd lined up around the biggest watermelon in the garden.

"Perfect timing," Joe said. "It'll be just right for the picnic."

"It looks like Tralice, lying in the sun," said Red. Joe snorted. Tralice had argued fiercely and in vain to be allowed to sunbathe on Sundays. But today she was with Aunt Phoebe, helping her finish a new sail for the *Kite*. No one had seen it yet but them.

The *Kite* herself already waited by the pier, freshly painted white with blue trim. But even that sight made Red feel no better.

"Are you moping, or sulking?" asked Uncle Herman, seeing Red's face as she sat on the back steps later that afternoon, staring out at the water.

Red thought for a minute. "Moping, I guess. I don't guess I have anything to sulk about."

"I'm relieved," Uncle Herman said.

"It's about the summer. I wish the Fourth

of July was in June, and then I could have it and the whole summer, too."

"Time goes fast," said Uncle Herman. "They say it goes faster as you get older, but I don't know that I agree. I remember childhood as being much too short, while it seems like I've been a grown-up forever . . . or at least I've been expected to act like one."

Red sighed. She wished people would stop talking about growing up. "If I were grown-up, I could tell everyone what to do."

"If I weren't grown-up, I could let everyone tell me what to do."

He sat down by her, and they both looked out at the bay for a long time without speaking.

"Blackberrying again tomorrow," Carrie Mae reminded Red that evening as they climbed the stairs to bed. She and Red had talked it over with Margaret Jones and decided to make blackberry cobbler for the picnic.

Red made an inarticulate sound of agreement, still brooding over the too-rapid approach of the Fourth of July. But in spite of herself, her heart lifted at the thought of the feast and the festivities. Uncle Herman would make new-potato salad with dill from the garden. Aunt

137

Phoebe would make pan-fried chicken. There would be biscuits and cornbread sticks and a hundred other things spread out on picnic tables joined together from one end of the Community Center grounds to the other. Games and contests would be held. And at the end of the day, she and her cousins would sail the *Kite* to the picnic, and afterward across the bay and back.

"I bet Joe doesn't decide he'd rather swim than eat that day!" Red then added, somewhat inaccurately, "He thinks Tralice looks like his watermelon sunbathing on tin cans!"

Carrie Mae snickered in spite of herself.

The Fourth of July arrived, hot and silver-blue. First thing that morning after breakfast, the family raised the flag at the end of the pier. Then Aunt Phoebe and Tralice brought out the sail.

The new sail was bright red, with thirteen white appliqué stars sprinkled in a curve like a new moon near the top. The sail fit exactly. It flapped slightly in the breeze.

"It's perfect." Carrie Mae jammed her hands hard in her pockets with emotion. "Perfect and beautiful."

"Like a flag on the water, to celebrate," said Red, with wholehearted admiration.

138

Even Tralice looked pleased. "It's not bad," she said.

"You'll make quite an entrance, sailing up to the picnic," said Aunt Phoebe.

Aunt Phoebe was so well organized that there was no flurry of last-minute things to be done. The food, in a picnic basket and neatly labeled shoeboxes, was stacked carefully in the back of the truck. Everyone's clothes had been made ready the night before. George was given a horse salad as a treat: carrots and apples mixed with a little sugar. Even the truck had been washed and polished.

Red and her cousins set off in the *Kite* right on time, sailing briskly before the wind to the Community Center. They anchored just off the point, beneath the Stars and Stripes the town flew there every day. Tablecloths weighted with food were already spread, and more were being added every minute. The smells and the sounds reached them even against the wind.

Aunt Phoebe and Uncle Herman had already started filling one of the tables. The tablecloth was spread and the truck half unloaded.

Every kind of dog imaginable seemed to be racing in and out, along with just as many young children. A baby moving with more de-

139

termination than speed toward a ball intended for a dog caught Red's eye for a moment. *It moves like Paint,* she thought.

Johnnie Brackett came over to show them the deviled eggs she'd made from a magazine recipe. She had swirled the fillings with a fork and stuck bits of parsley on each one.

Red looked the eggs over carefully. "Can you *eat* these?"

"Don't be—" Johnnie almost said "silly," but stopped in time. She smiled condescendingly instead. "Of course you can. *Do* try one."

"One for Carrie Mae, too," said Red.

"Please," said Tralice.

"Puh-lease," said Red.

"Honestly," Johnnie said. She gave Red two deviled eggs, and Red took one over to Carrie Mae and they picked the parsley off.

"Pretty good." Red was surprised. "You think Johnnie Brackett might amount to something?"

The general buzz of motion and noise stopped. Mayor Buttram stood on the top step of the Community Center, waving his hands.

"God bless America!" shouted the Mayor cheerfully. "We're going to pray, and then we're going to sing the national anthem—and then we're going to eat and have a few games in honor of this glorious day. God bless America!"

Red kept her head down dutifully during the prayer, but as everyone began to sing, "Oh, say can you seeee . . ." she elbowed Carrie Mae. By careful maneuvering and discreet sidling, they managed to be first in line as the anthem ended. In spite of that, they didn't get one of everything. But between them they got fried chicken, more deviled eggs, potato salad, cole slaw, creamed corn, string beans cooked with fatback, fried green tomatoes, fried okra, stewed tomatoes, oyster casserole, fried fish, biscuits, peach cobbler, blackberry cobbler, pecan pie, banana pudding, sweet-potato pie, and cold watermelon.

"My eyes wanted more than my stomach," Carrie Mae groaned, putting her plate down gingerly.

Red said, "I might have eaten too much," and put her plate down, too.

Joe crammed a last spoonful of banana pudding into his mouth. "Time for softball. Come on. You'll feel better if you move around. That's a proven fact."

"If it's a fact," said Red, "why do I feel like I'd rather stay here?"

Johnnie came over, and Tralice got up, too.

"Mrs. Shoemaker and I are shortly to make history in the three-legged race," said Uncle Herman. "You go on."

"I'm not shortly going to do anything if I can help it," said Red. "I wish I had four stomachs, like a cow."

"Yuck," Carrie Mae said. "Good-bye."

"One," said Uncle Herman, reaching down to pull Aunt Phoebe to her feet. "Even if we did have four stomachs, like cows, who's to say we wouldn't have four stomachaches? Two: At a picnic like this, even with the four stomachs of a cow, we'd still be pigs. Three: Why ask for four stomachs like a cow, niece, when it is readily apparent that you have that capacity normally attributed to the goat—I refer to your ability to eat everything!"

"Not everything," said Red. She looked down at her stomach. Any sort of motion did seem unwise. She settled herself more comfortably against the tree, and closed her eyes and listened to the sounds of the picnic. She heard the advice being shouted back and forth across the softball game, the cheers and jeers of the races. The general, steady hubbub filtered through the exhaustion wrought by her gluttony like a radio played at the other end of a house.

Joe poked her with his foot a while later. "Sooey, sooey, here, pigpigpig," he mocked her.

With her eyes still closed, Red stuck out her tongue. When she felt Joe go away, she opened them and looked down at her stomach again. It didn't look so distended. She felt better.

Joe was walking out toward the point. Tralice was already out there, and Carrie Mae, in her life jacket, was on her way toward Red, carrying another one.

Yawning and stretching, Red went over to the picnic tables. She took some leftover corn-sticks and biscuits and a piece of sweet-potato pie and wrapped them in napkins, just in case.

"You didn't miss much," said Carrie Mae, handing Red the life jacket. "Johnnie and Joe came in ahead of me and Tralice in the egg-and-spoon race. Joe claims they would have won if Johnnie hadn't made him laugh."

"You're right, I didn't miss much," Red said, looking up from the table. "Except the chess pie."

"We'll meet you back at our pier to watch

143

the fireworks," Aunt Phoebe said as they settled into the sailboat. "Don't be too long or you'll miss making ice cream." She gave the *Kite* a push.

" 'Would I could cast a sail on the water/ where many a king has gone/and many a king's daughter,' " quoted Uncle Herman.

"What's that?" asked Red.

"It's from a poem, 'The Collar-Bone of a Hare,' by William Butler Yeats, about a lost, magic world the poet wishes he could have again."

"Hare?"

"Rabbit, then," said Uncle Herman.

"What does a rabbit's collarbone have to do with anything?" Red asked.

"You can look it up when you get back."

"No thanks," Red called back hastily as Tralice turned the *Kite* to the edge of the wind.

Soon they were far, far out in the bay. The waves grew choppier, and the water foamed around the boat as it cut across the current.

"I've never seen our pier from way over here," said Red. "We've never sailed this way."

"It's a long way away," said Carrie Mae.

A few minutes later Joe spoke. "Look. You can see the bottom on this side now."

Red leaned over the side of the boat. Sure enough, they had sailed almost all the way across the bay.

"It looks the same. It's not different at all!" Red was disappointed.

"What did you expect?" asked Joe.

"I don't know. It should be different. It's just not what I expected, that's all."

Tralice turned the *Kite* parallel to the shore. They took turns at the rudder as they sailed, looking at the houses and boats, and the people on the piers, and the flags flying in different places at almost every house. Then they sailed a little ways back out and dropped anchor while they ate the pie and corn sticks Red had wrapped in the napkin. Joe had brought some of Johnnie's deviled eggs.

"She felt bad nobody ate them all, so I took the rest," he explained.

Tralice gave Joe one of her looks, but only said, "I wish it could be summer forever."

"Me too," said Red.

"If it was, we wouldn't have any Christmas," said Carrie Mae.

"But there wouldn't be any school either," Red reminded her.

"I like school," said Joe.

Tralice said, "Some people will do anything to be different."

"Anyway," said Carrie Mae, always the peacemaker, "you don't have to go to school forever."

Tralice lay back on the bow of the boat as if she were considering the idea. The talk lapsed, and Joe and Carrie Mae began to make biscuit pellets and drop them over the side for the fish. Red trailed her hand in the water. The shadow of it waved back and forth over the amber sand. She felt sad, and she didn't know why. The salt breeze grew less sticky and the sun touched the horizon.

"Time to go back," said Tralice. She sat up and flexed her arms. Joe hoisted the anchor.

But there was not enough wind to sail by. The water had become as smooth and opaque as the inside of a shell.

They got the oars out and took turns rowing, but it was slow going without oarlocks. And it was made harder because none of them were quite the same size or strength. The *Kite* went in uneven curves instead of straight. None of them had ever been stranded without wind for so long, and so far out before. When the sun went down, they weren't much closer to their shore. Dark swept rapidly across the water.

"Darn it!" said Tralice.

"Drat," amended Carrie Mae.

"What are we going to do?" Joe asked.

"I don't know what else we can do," said Tralice. "We'll probably just go out to sea on the tide and never be heard from again." She flung her oar down and folded her arms.

The first stars came out. The dark water moved under the boat as if it were breathing, and there was no place where the night ended and the water began. The distant noises of the shore made everything around the boat that much quieter.

"We could use a flashlight to signal for help," suggested Red.

"What flashlight?" Joe asked.

"Oh," said Red.

"Someone will come and get us sooner or later," Carrie Mae said.

"Yeah," agreed Joe. "We should be listening so we can shout in time so they don't run over us."

"Oh," said Red again, in a smaller voice.

"We'll try rowing some more," Tralice said.

The lights on the land seemed as small and

far away as the stars. Red strained her ears to hear an oncoming boat above the splash of the oars. But she heard only unfamiliar sounds, mysterious plunkings and slappings in the bay around them. She didn't trail her hand in the water.

KABOOM! KABOOM!

An explosion rocked the whole world. Red screamed and dove for the middle of the boat. When she screamed, everybody else screamed and jumped, too. The *Kite* swung back and forth wildly and almost tipped over.

KABOOM!

Red raised her head cautiously.

"The fireworks," she cried. "Oh, look, look!"

The Pine Level Community Center Fourth of July Fireworks had begun. The sky filled with webs and spangles of fiery light that spun toward their reflections in the water. The dark was gone.

They watched in silence as the flowers and umbrellas and pinwheels of color and light unraveled the night. As they watched, the night wind began to pick and puff the sail. In silence still, Tralice pulled the rope taut and began to tack home over the firework-phosphorescent water. The last wheel of light spun and faded as they sailed up to the pier.

Red never forgot that night. Always after,

she thought of that summer as a blue wave lit by the sun, with the Fourth of July at the crest of it. All summer long she had sailed up the wave, through the slow, fat, satisfying days with plenty of time to do everything that needed doing. Then the Fourth of July blazed and was gone and she rushed down the other side of the summer wave, like the *Kite*. The days burned up and blew away and vanished forever. Time went on and people changed and even the things that seemed important could fade away and be forgotten.

But as Tralice docked the boat that night, while Uncle Herman chanted, "Row, row, row your boat, last one out is a billy goat," and Aunt Phoebe laughed, and Joe said, "But we couldn't row at all!" and began to tell the whole story, Red, squeezing Carrie Mae's hand, had understood something else and was comforted.

Summer ends, she thought. *Summer ends, but it always comes again.*

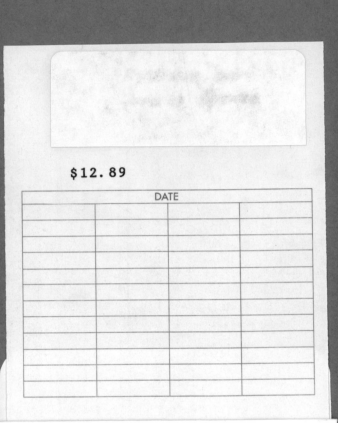

$12.89

DATE			